**Breaking the P.O.W.'s out took fire power.
Getting them home would take a miracle...**

"Mr. Stone, I really am uncomfortable around all these weapons. These men are strange. Two of them say they were prisoners of war until last night. Is that true?"

"Yes. We came to rescue them and bring them home. Our helicopter was shot down."

"All of this is illegal, I presume, from what little I know of you."

"Entirely illegal, Miss Filmore. The U.S. government has specifically forbid me from coming to the far east, and this country in particular. Does that bother you?"

"'Render unto Caesar,' Mr. Stone. 'Render unto Caesar.'"

M.I.A. HUNTER
EXODUS FROM HELL

JACK BUCHANAN

A JOVE BOOK

M.I.A. HUNTER: EXODUS FROM HELL

A Jove Book / published by arrangement with
the author

PRINTING HISTORY
Jove edition / February 1986

ISBN: 0-515-08544-8

Jove Books are published by The Berkley Publishing Group,
200 Madison Avenue, New York, N.Y. 10016.
The words "A JOVE BOOK" and the "J" with sunburst
are trademarks belonging to Jove Publications, Inc.

PRINTED IN THE UNITED STATES OF AMERICA

"Go with us as we seek to defend the defenseless and to free the enslaved."
—from the "Special Forces Prayer"

EXODUS FROM HELL

Chapter One

All around them lay the Cambodian jungle, dripping wet from a recent rain, and the eye could almost see it molding, rotting, decomposing its way back into the vegetation life cycle. The jungle had a smell all of its own, too: dampness, stagnant water, a mustiness of decaying leaves and fiber, the scent of microscopic life forms that breed and die, and the musk of larger animals that enter the pattern of kill or be killed.

Death for humans lay nearby, too.

Twenty feet ahead of Mark Stone, six Vietnamese regular troopers stepped back after having stripped the fresh corpses of three Cambodian civilians of their questionable valuables—watches, cheap jewelry, and a few odds and ends from shredded backpacks, the contents of which had been strewn across a small widening of this jungle trail.

To Stone the dead looked like peasant refugees, their sprawled corpses bayoneted: two adults, probably father and mother, and a teenage daughter whose nakedness indicated that she had probably been raped before being slaughtered by one or more of the Viet regulars whose snickering among themselves had alerted Stone and drawn him to observe soundlessly this moonlit tableau . . . too damn late to help the three unfortunate refugees who had been unable to escape the savagery of this Southeast Asian hellground.

Stone crouched there. His anger and hatred for the terrorists in military uniforms building to a white-hot killing anger inside his gut, he cursed the realization that not one of them could fire a shot. They were too close to the P.O.W. prison camp to take the chance of alerting anyone at the camp. Whatever they did now had to be a silent death.

He edged back from his O.P. and whispered with his P.O.W. hunter team, and they moved silently forward, swinging out to surround the wide place on the trail where the Viet patrol had caught up with the Cambodian family.

All the soldiers had pulled rice rolls from under their camouflage fatigue shirts. The inch-thick, two-foot long soft plastic tubes of precooked rice by themselves were enough to last a Vietnamese soldier in the field for a week. They began eating, unmindful of the three murder victims only a few feet away. Flies and insects quickly gathered at the blood feast. The soldiers did not notice.

Now was the time. Stone had not been able to save the lives of the innocent Cambodians, but he could make their killers pay the ultimate price. Each of Stone's highly trained, jungle combat specialists knew what to do.

AK-47's, the classic Russian automatic rifle with the 7.62mm round, lay close to each Vietnamese, but for the moment the weapons were ignored. The kill was forgotten. Eager hands scooped rice into hungry mouths.

The sergeant of this Viet scavenger patrol, a Tokarev 9mm pistol holstered at his hip, appeared the most alert of the six to Stone who observed the Viet Army noncom staring at the jungle gloom around them from time to time. These murderous military bandits continued eating, chuckling among themselves as if the three butchered remains of their victims were not sprawled a few feet away.

Stone knew this noncom must be important if he had been issued a Russian pistol favored by the KGB.

Stone checked his watch. The six other fighting men on his team would be in position. They were close by, set at strategic points in a circle around the six Vietnamese and each one assigned a specific target. One of his men lay behind the big teak tree that soared more than a hundred feet into the sky and helped form the top of a natural canopy. To the left, near the betel palm, waited Hog Wiley. A thicket of small bamboo screened the other side of the small clearing.

Stone let the Viet soldiers relax a little more. His team had no choice but to hit this patrol, even though it was so close to their objective. It had to be silent because they were less than a mile from a reported M.I.A. prison camp. This was the only way down a narrow gorge without backtracking five miles and going around. That would make them late for their chopper pickup after they rescued the P.O.W.'s.

It had to be a hit—now and without a sound, no word spoken or shot fired.

Stone was a big man, an inch over six feet, with heavily muscled shoulders and legs and a tapered waist that gave no display of extra fat. He weighed 210 pounds and was as hard as old shoe leather. His eyes were a deadly blue-gray. Stone had on a black headband around his black hair, wore a Marine tank-top undershirt in the tropical oven, fatigues, and a combat pack. Across his pack was tied a SPAS-12 automatic shotgun loaded with eight rounds of double-ought buck.

Stone was glad he had brought the Beretta 93-R with him. He had screwed the short, fat silencer on its nose, and he now lifted the small automatic and sighted in past bamboo at the sergeant with the pistol. The coughing sound of the silencer would be the attack signal.

He aimed just over the Vietnamese murderer's nose and squeezed off the round. The 9mm Parabellum ran straight and true, blasting in an inch below the man's hairline, taking the top of his head off as it blew him backward into the edge of the dense jungle.

Hog Wiley lay in the wet muck barely containing his power and energy. He was well over six feet tall, a powerful, bearlike figure and the ugliest man Mark Stone had ever seen. He was a bearded, straggle-haired behemoth and a good old boy from East Texas who could dirt-track race with the best but preferred the animal survival tactics of a destruction derby.

Now, Wiley was poised to strike. He heard the sound of the silencer come through the chatter of the Viets and saw one of the enemy slam backward.

He silently drove forward the six yards to his assigned target, a small Vietnamese who carried a backpack probably filled with grenades and explosives, items they could use.

Hog snarled as he pounded ahead, the big eight-inch blade of his double-sided fighting knife out in front of him like a saber. He could see more of his buddies charging into the Viets, but then there was no time to think of the others. His target dropped his rice and dived to one side after his rifle.

Hog adjusted his attack angle and in another two steps had plowed into the writhing, squirming Oriental. The big knife got there first, jamming into the Viet's belly, ramming upward eight inches, then severing the aorta from the heart and dumping the Viet soldier into his own personal heaven or hell.

The big man from Texas jerked the fighting knife from the corpse and spun around, ready to defend himself or help others.

To his left, a machete-wielding friend had missed with the first killing blow. The big blade had hacked off the enemy soldier's right arm, but he grabbed at his rifle with his left, his finger reaching for the trigger.

One gunshot could abort Stone's whole rescue mission!

Hog surged toward the fighting pair. The soldier's finger gained the trigger housing just as Hog stomped his size-twelve boot down on his arm jolting the weapon away from him and bringing a anguished cry of pain.

As Hog looked up, the Cambodian anti-Communist guer-rilla and member of Stone's team swung the machete again. The big American saw the terrified look in the Vietnamese fighter's eyes. His left hand tried to lift to defend himself, but it was still pinned under Hog's boot.

The machete came down like a scythe through rice stalks, decapitating the trooper in one blow. Hog looked with a new sense of appreciation at the slight Cambodian helper, and then checked for other action.

Terrance Loughlin, the red-haired Englishman who had been a demolitions expert with the Special Air Service Com-mandos, charged like a light brigade when he heard the sigh of the silencer and saw its target flail backward. Loughlin's assignment was the man carrying a knee mortar.

The Brit held a hatchet in his right hand and a four-inch, razorlike blade in his left. He slipped on his first step, growled, and drove harder the six more strides he needed after jolting from behind the betel palm.

His enemy lifted both feet to fend off the rushing man in front of him. He pawed for his big AK-47, but this was infighting, and there was no space to maneuver the long gun to get off a shot.

Loughlin swung the hatchet from the side; the sharp blade struck the Viet's upthrust left leg just above the ankle break-ing both bones and bringing a wail of anguish from the squirming, snarling killer and rapist.

The English commando surged silently past the legs, the hatchet already recocked in his strong right hand, and as he dived forward he swung the weapon.

It *thunked* into the enemy skull like a knife going into a ripe watermelon. The Vietnamese soldier's eyes blazed for a moment, then the fire went out of them. A last sigh escaped the pursed lips, for the soldier had paid the ultimate price.

Loughlin yanked his death hatchet from the corpse's skull. Two of the team's Cambodian anti-Communist guerrillas were struggling with a larger Vietnamese. He had a pistol out and fisted but could not point it at the smaller Cambodians.

Loughlin bolted eight feet to the battle, grabbed the Viet's hand, and forced it back toward the man's own head. Then, he found room between the Cambodians and swung the bloody hatchet down again. The blade slashed through the man's forehead and halfway through his brain.

Mark Stone holstered the silenced Beretta and looked over the battlefield. The fourth Cambodian guerrilla on his team was locked in a knife fight with a Viet who had lost his rifle. Stone ran across the six yards and executed a frontal snap-kick hard against the Viet's kidney area, spinning him around.

Stone then used his forearm to block the swipe of the blade. The Viet now ignored the Cambodian and concentrated on the tougher opponent.

The Viet tried a kick that missed. It gave Stone a chance to step inside it and throw a spearhead blow with stiffened fingers aimed for the solar plexus. It also missed. But then Stone followed with a spinning back fist, which surprised the Viet and caught him just below the jaw. The snapping crack of his jawbone breaking sounded loud in the darkened silence.

They circled each other a moment, the Viet still threatening with his knife. Stone faked another spinning blow, then struck suddenly with a frontal snap-kick that broke the Viet's right wrist and spun the knife into the jungle greenery.

The Vietnamese killer screamed into the night.

Stone surged forward with a leaping kick, smashing his toe into the Viet's voice box, cutting off the scream. The Viet sagged, holding his throat and gasping for breath.

The big American jolted forward, lifted his right hand,

and came down with an elbow strike at the base of the Vietnamese's skull. His elbow broke the soldier's neck and he slumped into the trail, dead. He rolled over staring upward at the second canopy of greenery shielding the dark trail.

Six, Stone thought to himself. He stood in the trail panting, checking each of his men.

Stone's force had frozen in place. Now, they checked around them. All six of the Vietnamese were dead. Mark signaled his men to pick up any grenades and explosives. His team was armed with CAR-15's, the chattering fully automatic rifles with .223 stingers much like the army's M-16, only they were shorter and lighter.

He looked at the AK-47's the Vietnamese carried. It was the best rifle the Russians ever made. It might not be a bad idea to grab one of the heavier weapons and take it along—might have a special need for one.

The men threw the enemy rifles deep into the jungle on both sides of the clearing. Stone saved one of the AK-47's and four curved magazines of the 7.62mm rounds.

Loughlin had made a quick search of the bodies and packs, but he found no radio. He looked at the pack containing the explosives, saw that they all were U.S. made grenades, and slung it over his right shoulder.

The men stood watching their leader, waiting.

Not a word had been spoken.

He gave the infantry signal for moving forward: his hand in the air, waving the men ahead.

They had another mile to negotiate through the darkness of the Cambodian jungle. It would be slow going, but they had over a half hour to reach their objective.

Mark Stone let part of himself relax as he led the small band through the forest and down a semblance of a trail. He prayed that the three M.I.A.'s would still be there and that they would be healthy enough to walk out of the compound and the estimated eight miles back to the LZ.

Stone knew he had to get them out. If An Khom said there were three G.I.'s in here, they would be here. The wily underground arms dealer in Bangkok, who supplied Stone with his hardware, was seldom wrong on his intel about P.O.W.'s.

Mark Stone was betting his life that he could get them out.

Stone wanted to rescue them more than anything, perhaps more than life itself.

He knew what a Vietnamese P.O.W. camp was like. Near the end of the war he had done time in a North Vietnamese prisoner of war camp. It had been a living nightmare that would haunt him for as long as he lived: bamboo cages built to imprison the Americans so that they could neither fully stand up nor lie down; vicious, brutal guards who beat prisoners for recreation; subhuman meals that rotted long-term prisoner's vitality; work loads that broke dozens of men who were not as big or as strong as Stone; the agony of believing that your country had forgotten you and no way to be sure; the depressing on-display parades through villages and towns where captured prisoners were scorned, spat on, and poked with sharp bamboo sticks.

Near the end of the war, the Viets had listed Stone and some others as prisoners so they could have the publicity of releasing him and a few others to mask the hundreds they made no mention of. There could be *thousands* of prisoners over here, unreported even after ten long years. He knew this based on hard—very hard—experience.

Miraculously, he had been freed. When he returned home he was asked to re-enlist and was offered a commission. He told them about other P.O.W.'s the Viets had not listed and who were hidden away deep in the jungles of Laos, Cambodia, and Vietnam. The government did not believe him.

He was angered, worried, and then disillusioned with the government and the army when they would not commit any action to rescue his comrades who had risked their lives in a call to fight for their country.

It had been an unpopular war that politicians and leaders wanted to forget, to put behind them. The P.O.W. and M.I.A. causes simply forced them to recall the war and how we lost, and the American government had refused to touch either problem.

Stone was not a wealthy man, yet the only charges he ever made to M.I.A. relatives were for his bare expenses— *if* he came back with the missing man and only if the family could afford it. It was no way to get rich.

But he knew Indochina. He knew the military. He had been a master sergeant in the Green Berets, stationed at Da Nang during much of the war. He was an expert in covert actions, such as border-crossing operations into Laos, Cambodia, and North Vietnam. He also did hit and run missions.

Since he was a Green Beret, he had taken extensive training in infiltration, demolition, hand-to-hand combat, weapons, survival, camouflage, and being a paratrooper.

Stone spent more tours of duty in Vietnam than any other Green Beret. It made him at home in the entire region, since he knew the languages, the people, their politics, and the terrain of that end of the world that was at once lush and deadly. He was by necessity an expert at survival in the green hell of the Oriental jungles where he had been on his own dozens of times and had to live off the country.

He had been successful bringing back G.I.'s wherever he found them—whether or not someone had hired him to go looking.

He kept an extremely low profile. No mention was made when a G.I. was discovered and returned. That would only bring more surveillance from the International Security Affairs Division. That outfit was the host agency to the Defense Security Assistance Agency which dealt, or rather did not deal, directly with the M.I.A. problem according to its ever-changing and delicate political instructions.

So the only spread of the gospel of Mark Stone's bringing back M.I.A.'s was by word-of-mouth from one mother or wife or other relative to another. But it was enough. He knew that few chances to free discovered M.I.A.'s would slip past him.

Hog and Terrance formed the heart of his liberation force, but he had a roster of some thirty men he could call on who would work for expenses to rescue M.I.A.'s. These men were mercenaries who worked for big dollars elsewhere, but to bring out long-held P.O.W.'s, they would risk their lives for nothing.

Sometimes government data helped. Stone had a pipeline directly into the Defense Department. Her name was Carol Jenner and she was an intelligence processor with the department. She was also tall and beautiful, a blonde with more than a touch of class . . . and she was tough. She had blue eyes that had been seeing only Mark Stone lately. She was more beauty queen than Hollywood could handle, smarter than computers, and lots more fun in bed.

If something unusual or attractive showed up in governmental data about M.I.A. sightings, she quickly and safely passed the intel on to Mark Stone. He knew exactly how to use it, and so far there had been no problems for Carol.

He knew when he began that he could not go on such missions by himself. He needed reliable side men and backup. He had been well known in the small, international community of soldiers of fortune. During the last few missions he had concentrated on Loughlin and Wiley and the operations had gone smoothly. It was his core team but he had experts he could call on when he needed them.

Now, it was time for action. He stopped the team and squinted ahead through a fringe of trees at the camp hovering in a sudden splash of floodlights three hundred yards away.

Stone did not care if the government said there was no more M.I.A. problem. He did not care if the Vietnamese would not cooperate in finding graves or bones of G.I.'s, including those killed in P.O.W. camps.

All he cared about right now was moving into that target, finding out if there were any G.I.'s there, taking them out, and sending them home to their families. That was his job, and he was going to do it, no matter what government agencies told him to do!

He slid to the ground and stared past a screen of bamboo at the lighted P.O.W. camp directly ahead.

Chapter Two

Stone had been spending a few days of R&R in Bangkok when he had a note to contact An Khom, the aging arms dealer with whom Stone did business. Mark had taken three taxis, walked four blocks to be sure no one followed him, then slipped into the pagoda, and eased down the semidarkness of the central aisle to the altar.

An Khom had greeted him there and took him into a back room where he fixed tea, served it, and only then got down to business.

"Mr. Stone, we have received interesting news of three Americans in a P.O.W. camp deep in Cambodia, well across the Mekong. They are in a work camp. The sightings have been made by two different observers who could not benefit from lying."

Stone had felt his scalp tingle. Three more!

"How current is this information?"

"Two, maybe three weeks. But the watchers said it apparently is a permanent camp, carved out of the jungle. There is little work to be done in that place, so it may only be a jail."

"If you're that positive, we have to go in." Stone's tingle turned into surging excitement. A chance to get more long-time P.O.W.'s out of Viet hands!

The old Thai's face lit with pleasure. "I am glad. To serve one's fellow man is the greatest calling a person can have."

"I won't have a sponsor, no expense money..."

"That has been part of my consideration. We will play a gambling game, you and I... double or nothing."

"Double?"

"I will furnish the materials for the trip two hundred miles into Cambodia. If the Americans are there and you bring them out, and if any can pay for the expenses, perhaps from back wages, or one's family can pay..." An Khom knew a U.S. serviceman could have an extremely large paycheck coming after ten years without pay.

"Then we pay you double the usual costs," Stone filled in.

The wrinkled, ancient Thai smiled and his eyes almost closed.

"It is a small wager. It is, in part, my debt to you for rescuing my only daughter when bandits attacked and destroyed my home."

Stone stood quickly and held out his hand.

"Deal. I've got to move quickly to stop Loughlin and Wiley from heading to the States."

An Khom smiled again. "No need. I contacted both of them and told them you would want to see them today and that they may need to cancel their trips eastward."

Stone settled back in the rattan chair and sipped the delicious green tea that An Khom had poured.

"You figured I would take your proposition."

An Khom laughed softly and with it came the wisdom that seemed so natural to an Oriental.

"Mr. Stone. I thought you might refuse the double or

nothing offer, but if you had I would have countered with a normal expenses offer—to be paid only if the rescued G.I.'s could afford it. You see I am a sentimentalist. There is honor among men like us."

An hour later Hog Wiley had shouldered his way into the small room in the back of the pagoda, and he and Stone went together for the needed arms and radios from the new warehouse An Khom had established. Terrance was not at his hotel, but he had not checked out. Stone knew where to find the Brit, and he knew that the delicate Chinese girl he would be with would cry a new river of tears as Terrance slipped away from her arms.

The next day they met at a small commercial airfield near Bangkok. The chopper they would use had been painted during the night to look like a camouflaged Vietnamese army bird. It was a Huey, the kind the Viets captured from the U.S. when we pulled out.

The four anti-Communist Cambodian guerrillas An Khom recommended were on hand. They would complete the attack team. One spoke good English; the others were quick and understood the mission and its importance. They looked forward to killing as many of the hated, invading, butchering Vietnamese as they could.

The Americans stared at the map. They would land wells south of the Cambodian city of Stung Treng. It was 240 air miles from the Thai border.

They loaded their gear, and just as dusk closed over the city, they took off heading for the Cambodian border.

They soon charged over the city of Aranyaprathet, Thailand on the border with Cambodia. Then, they were over enemy territory and could be attacked at any time.

The plan was to fly to the LZ in darkness and drop off the rescue team. Stone and his men would have plenty of time to get to the target by midnight since it was nearby.

"That's to hell and gone over there," Hog had grumbled.

"One bitch of a walk home if anything happens to our transport," Terrance said. "That's on the other side of the Mekong!"

"True, not the easiest mission we've had," Stone grunted. "But the intel is that there are three Americans in there."

"Shit, let's hit them!" Hog said.

"Hell, in for a pence, in for a pound." Loughlin nodded.

"You say these guys went down in a B-52 back in seventy-three?" Hog asked.

"How can anyone live for thirteen years in one of those camps?" Terrance wondered aloud.

"We're learning more about the P.O.W. camps each time we bring someone out. Lately, the Viets seem to be moving the prisoners around every year or so. It cuts down the chance of making local contacts or getting to know the local countryside. Some of the guys we've brought out said they were even in Hanoi for a while, the old Hanoi Hilton. I guess a change of scenery would help some guys to hang on to hope."

Terrance shook his head. "Christ! Thirteen fucking years! Can you believe that? Thirteen years in a cage?"

There had been massive changes in the political and military situation in the old Indochina since the end of the Vietnam war. Stone knew that the Vietnamese had continued their stranglehold on Laos, the long, thin nation directly to its west. Cambodia had been taken over by the Khmer Rouge after the Vietnamese hostilities ended, and in a year the new government created havoc with the whole nation— shipping city people to the country, uprooting rural men and women and families and sending them to the city.

It was a dictatorial, savage regime that some historians say killed more than a million of the seven million people then living in Cambodia. One in seven!

The Vietnamese government had been consolidating its hold on all of Vietnam and Laos and then looked west and gobbled up Cambodia with its military might fragmenting the opposition. By now only the Khmer Rouge was left as a guerrilla force opposing the Viets. Their forces had been chopped down dramatically after their mountain headquarters, Phnom Malai near the Thai border, was captured.

Now Vietnam controlled all of the vast territory that was the old French Indochina. Its leaders' one big worry was a half million Chinese troops just across their 500-mile long northern border. Vietnam kept an equal force facing the monster to the north, as the Viets referred to China.

In this area, anywhere outside of Thailand was considered enemy territory. As the chopper sped along over hills and along valleys and streams, Stone realized how far it would be to walk out if something went sour the chopper. They had never been this deep into enemy territory before.

What if their intel was faulty?

What if their supposed friends inside Cambodia doublecrossed them?

The basic transport plan was simple. Fly in at night, deplane at the LZ, and the chopper would fly a bit deeper into the wilderness to a spot where it could be concealed under freshly cut green brush until it was needed.

At the appointed time, dawn, it would fly back to the LZ, pick up the team and the three M.I.A.'s, and scramble for Thailand, hoping that the daylight run could be made on the strength of the Vietnamese chopper's paint job.

Simple.

Dangerous.

Terrance had been briefing the English-speaking Cambodian on every aspect of the mission he could presently devise. The Cambodian would, in turn, translate the information to his three countrymen.

Stone listened to the Cambodian translate for a few minutes until he was satisfied that the right words were being used. He could understand the language much better than speak it.

The pilot, a blustering Irishman who had hooked up with

An Khom nearly five years before, found the LZ with no trouble. It was near a perfect V made by two streams joining. The water made a silvery outline in the moonlight. No lights and no buildings could be seen in any direction.

The landing was routine, and Terrance and Hog had apportioned the supplies, including CAR-15 magazines and explosives, into each of the seven packs, putting less in the smaller Cambodian's.

They stepped to the ground and moved out quickly into the cover of the heavy jungle fifty yards away. The landing pad turned out to be a dry rice paddy that would soon be flooded for the rice crops to begin again.

Mark took the lead, aiming the short file into the brush and jungle. Once there, he paused to orient himself, and then with his compass in hand, he struck off nearly due east, searching for a trail that supposedly ran from this river to the camp.

Quickly, he changed plans. The jungle was impossible to work through without some kind of trail. Instead, they walked along the edge of the clearing near the rice paddies until he found a cart trail that soon turned east and, Stone hoped, toward the camp.

As Stone passed one of the Cambodians, he bumped him and the person's cap fell off. Luxuriant, long black hair cascaded out. Mark groaned and stared at the trooper in the faint moonlight coming through the light growth.

One Cambodian was a woman, not a man, and she was the one who spoke English!

She quickly put her hair back under the hat and looked up, tension and some fear on her face.

"Why?" Stone asked her.

"My husband die from Communist. I get them for it. I fight good. I learn years ago. I am good fighter. I need money for two babies. I come and fight and help!"

Stone had been at the back of the file. He let the others

go on ahead. He would not tell them yet. If she could fight, fine. At least, she could translate. He hoped that the traditional Oriental modesty would prevent any other problems.

He touched her shoulder.

"I understand. Do your Cambodians know?"

She nodded. "One is my brother."

"Great. We won't tell the two Americans yet. Okay?"

"Okay."

They hurried to catch up with the others and Stone moved her inside the line so she would not be at the end where there could be trouble.

This mission wasn't starting out right. More than two hundred miles from friendly ground and he now had a woman guerrilla as one of his fighters! He had taken women along before, never by choice.

Hell, maybe it would all be downhill from here.

They hiked for an hour and Stone figured they had covered half the distance. His watch showed that it was 2030 hours. They had until midnight to get set up for the attack. That would leave them plenty of time for the return march for the 0630 hours departure from the LZ. That was the plan and he hoped they could stick to it.

Stone was leading the line now, and he stopped, his nose twitching, sniffing.

Smoke.

He had smelled no smoke for hours. Now, there were traces of smoke on the wind. Smoke meant people and people out here meant trouble for this team.

They moved cautiously, slower, and a short distance ahead they came upon a sleeping village that straddled the trail. A small stream swept by it and there were two rice paddies. There were a dozen thatched huts. Logs slanted up to the floors, which were built four feet off the ground. The logs had cross-pieces on them to form steps.

Stone sent Terrance through first. He saw nothing, heard nothing. Two chickens moved reluctantly out of the way as he passed. He shrugged and waved the others forward. He had found no traps or surprises.

Stone sent the people through two at a time after that, and he brought up the rear. He didn't relax until they were well down the trail.

He worked to the front of the line just as Terrance held up his hand and they all stopped and went down on one knee, rifles poised.

There was something ahead that meant big trouble and Stone had to find out what it was.

He flattened out beside Terrance at the side of the trail and observed the tableau of the very recently murdered Cambodian civilians and their murderers, a scavenging Viet patrol babbling among themselves with the excitement of the kills and what had gone with it.

"No way around," Terrance whispered to Stone. "We'd get lost out there in this bloody jungle. Those hills back there mean we have to go through these rapists."

"Yeah, but silently," growled Stone. "That P.O.W. camp is less than a mile away. Any firefight this close would alert everyone within five miles. We have to take these scum out, but without making a sound."

Which is exactly what they proceeded to do.

Chapter Three

Something stung his cheek.

Sergeant Phil Patterson tried to turn over. He couldn't, there wasn't enough room. He tried to stretch his legs to get a better sleeping position.

Then he came wide awake and remembered.

He was in the suspended punishment box.

He was naked. He was cramped in a bamboo cage three feet long, two feet wide, and two feet high. He could not lie down; he could not sit up, he could only curl and hope for sleep or the bite of some poisonous snake. Maybe an Asian Two-Step, would climb the tree, then slither down the rope, come into the box, and bite him.

They used to call them Asian Two-Step because the blue-gray krait was so poisonous that after being bitten you supposedly would take only two steps before you died.

Sometimes he wished he could die.

How long had it been? Damn it, how long?

Quickly Patterson began singing. It was "The Yellow Rose of Texas," the only song he knew all the way through.

He sang it softly the first time, then louder until the guard on duty below fired three shots into the air from his AK-47 rifle.

Hon was on duty tonight. He would not risk hitting the basket and killing the prisoner. Only the bloody bastard Chau Tran, the camp commander, could kill a prisoner.

After the song he whispered his small prayer: "I'm gonna live through today and, damn it, live through tonight. Please, God, let somebody know about my plight!"

He said it over and over. Each time he moved, the cage swayed. It hung twenty feet in the air between two big teak trees. He forgot now what it was he did that they put him there. He was naked and cold right through to his bones.

To the Vietnamese, being naked in public was the greatest shame, the biggest loss of face or self that could happen to a person. He had done a damn lot of naked time.

The rain came. He cried for a minute, then stopped. That was dumb. He was too old to cry. That made him remember that he didn't know how old he was. He knew he was almost twenty when he went down with the plane. Or did he parachute? Yes, he hit the silk with three others. One of them, the lieutenant, broke his neck coming through the canopy. But good old Phil Patterson had made it fine—had lived so he could have eight, nine years of terror, brutality, and torture.

Damn, he wished the rain would stop!

Patterson grinned. Shit, he had given the little bastards a bad time today. He didn't remember what it was, but it was so much work for them to hoist him up here that it must have been fine!

He was six feet four, lots taller than the gooks. They hated him for that.

He was stronger than the little slant-eyes. They hated him for that.

He could work twice as hard as any of the other prisoners.

They hated him for that.

But they kept him alive. He was their prize. He didn't know why. Yes, yes he did know. Somehow Lieutenant Tran found out about his father, that he was in San Francisco and rich. Twice a week Tran offered Phil a big meal and wine. To get the food, all he had to do was sign a letter to his father asking for a million dollars in ransom for the release of his son.

Again and again over the years, Phil had refused to sign the letter. He tore most of them up and threw them in Tran's face. That meant more beatings, more cage, more nude time. He didn't care. He would never sign the letter!

He told Tran that if one more American prisoner died in camp that he would never, never, never sign the damn ransom letter. Things got a little better after that. But they were down to only three Americans.

Lightning lit the sky for a moment and the rains came down, drenching him again. Through the rain he sang two more verses of "The Yellow Rose of Texas" and Hon did not shoot at him.

Then, the rain stopped and he prayed again: "I'm gonna live through today and, damn it, I'm gonna live through tonight! Please God, let somebody know about my plight!"

He remembered then why they had beat him with the bamboo sticks and rammed him in the cage. He had been working on a ditch to bring water from the stream down to a series of small rice paddies. The Viet leader, a little bastard called Loc, had walked too close and the spade Phil used accidentally hit one of Loc's boots and he stumbled and fell in the irrigation ditch.

"Beautiful," Phil said out loud. "It was beautiful." The little Vietnamese had come out of the water sputtering, wiping the water from his face, coughing, and blowing his nose. When he recovered he drew his pistol, but the other guards would not let him shoot Phil. If he killed Phil, all the guards would be fined a whole year's pay. They had to keep the prisoners alive, especially this one. Tran had an unusual interest in this big one, Patterson.

After tripping the guard into the ditch, Phil had been stripped naked and led back to the village where his hands were tied behind him and the old men came up and spat on him. A toothless old woman kicked him and knocked him down; then they squatted and pissed on him. All the time he was laughing and calling the women whores. That was when they began hitting him with clubs and the guards ran in and made them stop.

He yahooed at the guards all the way back to camp, even as they kept pounding him with the bamboo.

Christ, he would like to kill every bamboo plant in Cambodia, or Laos, or Vietnam, wherever the hell he was now. He had been moved around to so many camps he couldn't keep track of them. Now, he was back here with Captain Carlson and Corporal Doug Hillburton, the other guys who survived that damn B-52 crash. It was chance he was at this camp again. No. Hell, no! Tran wanted him back for another chance at the ransom. The bloody little bastard would get his some day.

A sudden burning pain knifed through his gut and he screamed. It was as if a long, thin piece of bamboo had been jammed into his stomach and come out his back. He felt his belly, but there was no blood, no wound.

Hon, the guard below, laughed and called him a sick bird who couldn't even fly. Then, Hon shouted a string of obscenities in Vietnamese.

Sleep? Why couldn't he go to sleep? Usually he was so exhausted after working in the ditches all day that he went to sleep at once. This had been such an unusual day that he was still jazzed up. It was like the first time he got a real girl and she wanted to, too, and they undressed each other. Damn, but it had been great! He never knew sex could be so wild, so wonderful. After he finally took Sally home, he lay awake all night, just thinking about how fine, how beautiful, how marvelous it had been! He had seen Sally several times after his first evening with her.

That was it. He had to think about home—about the big house back in San Francisco and the parties they used to have, magical parties with bands and entertainers. Once the governor came and even the vice president! He couldn't remember which one. He knew it wasn't Nixon.

The knifing pain lanced through his gut and he screamed again. He had no idea what was happening. He urinated through the bars of the cage, but that didn't help. Fringes of the pain were still there.

He would go on sick call in the morning. Hell, if he were back in the good old U.S.A., he'd go in for sick call like a shot! Damn right. Couldn't work a guy when he was sick. He'd told his sergeant that three times just after basic and went on sick call. Then somehow his records got lost and he missed getting paid the next payday. Oh, they made it up, but his pay was a month late catching up. He never went on sick call again while he had that same sergeant. He had learned his lesson.

Captain Carlson sure looked bad. The little guy had guts; he would give him that. But you had to know how far to push these slant-eyed gooks. You couldn't insult them too much or they just went wild crazy and would beat you to death. Hell, maybe that was the answer.

Carlson got it bad today. He said he'd been having a lot of blood in his urine lately and he couldn't keep any food down. That was the first sign. Carlson might not make it more than a week, hard telling. If he gave up, if he refused to go to work tomorrow, he would be on a damn short fuse. Phil had a bad feeling about his making it.

One day at a time.

He had to keep living one day at a time.

"I'm gonna live through today and, damn it, live through tonight! Please, God, let somebody know about my plight!" He said the words aloud and then began to sing. From somewhere, he remembered the words and tune to "Red River Valley." That was a song his father used to sing—said he was a farm hand and learned the song from another guy who had a guitar, one with strings and no PA system behind it. Real music, his dad used to say. Then, he got off the farm and into town and made some good moves, and first thing he knew he was a millionaire. Lately he didn't know how much he was worth, probably four or five times what he had been then.

"Air Force?" his father had thundered. "Four years out of your life? I already fought the war for this family, you don't need to go. I can talk to the draft board; I can put the word in. I contribute enough to these damn political campaigns. They owe me."

Phil had enlisted the day after he graduated from high school. He was eighteen. He was eighteen, green, and dumb and thought he was hot shit!

Phil screamed into the night again. A muscle cramp—like on the track squad that last spring in high school. That had been fun, a damn hard workout, but fun. He could barely get to his calf now to rub it.

He dozed and woke with a start. The calf muscle again. He rubbed it out. It was the same leg the gooks had punished that first week after they crashed. The crash. That had been a once in a lifetime experience.

Phil remembered it like it was yesterday. They had come down from a high altitude bombing run. Nobody ever figured out what the problem was with their bird, but she was going down. The skipper said hit the silk and he did, just as the captain went out. The others had left earlier. Phil never heard what happened to them—whether they were captured or died in the jump?

He came through an opening in the top canopy and spilled enough air to hit the lower canopy only a dozen feet off the ground. He got down with no sweat and then there were twenty Vietcong women facing him, circling around him. They all had pointed bamboo sticks and began moving closer and closer. He had the .45 on his hip, but he wasn't about to shoot defenseless women.

Defenseless? Ha! They showed how defenseless they were. The first one jabbed him in the leg, then another tried and he shot into the ground in front of her. One got him in the back, just a nick, and by that time an AK-47 stuttered a dozen rounds over their heads. The women flattened on the ground and two Viet regulars came up with weapons aimed at his belly. He was almost glad to see them!

They stripped off his shirt, pants, and boots. They tied his hands behind him. Then, the women ripped off his G.I. shorts and broke up laughing. One of the regulars tied a thin piece of wire around his scrotum, cinched it tight, wound out twenty feet of wire, and gave a small tug.

Phil thought his balls were coming off! He had never experienced such intense, agonizing pain! He screeched in terror and surged forward to stop the pain. The Vietnamese soldier grunted and walked down a trail toward some kind of camp. Whenever Phil slowed, a tug on the wire propelled him along faster.

That's when he wished he'd killed all the Vietcong women he could have with the seven rounds in his .45 autoloader. They might have killed him, too, right then and saved him ten years of torture.

Damn, but it was getting cold. More rain showers coming. He looked at the small patch of stars he could see through the trees, but it told him nothing. He guessed it was about midnight, maybe not quite midnight.

Hell, if he made it through tonight, tomorrow he would think about everything before he said it. Maybe he could keep from being beaten up so much and stay out of the damn swaying cage. He longed for his nice big, roomy bamboo hut, the five-by-five cube that meant he could at least lie down by just bending his knees and scrunching up a little. It was a dozen ways better than the bird cage.

Christ, wouldn't this night ever end? Maybe tomorrow. Maybe by tomorrow somebody would find out he was here. Hell, yeah, just maybe. But don't hold your damn breath!

Chapter Four

Stone, Loughlin, and Hog Wiley lay fifty yards from the P.O.W. compound and timed the guards. It was a much smaller camp than any of them had anticipated. The whole thing was not more than forty yards square. Watchtowers, twenty feet high, had been built on two of the four corners. Lights from these points bathed the camp in a kind of big city atmosphere.

"The prisoner cages are in the center," Stone said. He had field glasses at his eyes. "I see six cages but I only see a man in one of them. Three are screened off."

"Looks like the generator shack is that one to the left, the only one with several lights burning inside," Loughlin said. "I can get to it with a preset charge and blast it whenever you say."

"Go set the charge," Stone said patting him on the back. He ran to the left, then into the heavy growth around the camp so he could work in behind the generator shack.

Someone in the camp began singing.

"What is that?" Hog asked.

Stone grinned. "That's "Red River Valley." No Vietnamese ever heard of that song. We've got at least one American in there!"

"Where's it coming from?" Hog asked. "Sounds up high somewhere."

Stone swung the glasses up. The light-gathering effect of regular binoculars surprises most people. Stone had long ago accepted the idea and used the principle as he scanned the trees. He spotted the cage and passed the glasses over to Hog.

"That's got to be our songbird. Your job, Hog, is to get him down without damage. Must be a rope on one of the two trees and a pulley. Sooner the better."

"I'm gone," Hog said, sliding away from the ridge and moving into the jungle growth more quickly and quietly than it seemed possible for a man of his size.

Stone placed all four of the Cambodians in base fire support. He told the Cambodian woman exactly what he wanted them to do. She listened closely.

"Hit everything that moves outside of our entrance and our exit lanes," he told her. "Our team will get into the cages in the center, clear them, bring out the M.I.A.'s and we may need some back-up and covering fire as we retreat to you."

She nodded, then repeated to him almost verbatim what he had said.

"If a target is bigger than the average Indochinese, don't fire at it," Stone said. "It probably will be one of us. And we don't know how many American P.O.W.'s there are in there. All four of your people are here, so we don't have to worry about ID in there. It's safer that way."

"Yes, understand," she said.

"We have the one AK-47 and four magazines of ammo. Use it and the CAR-15's. I want you to shoot up a bitching storm. When the generator shack blows, you should start firing. You understand?"

She grinned. "Big boom, then we shoot."

Stone moved up to the point of departure he and his two men had agreed on and waited. Loughlin was there within two minutes, grinning.

"Ready, mate, anytime you want her blown."

"We've got a man up a tree." Stone told him about the cage and they both watched as it lowered a little at a time. Then it came down suddenly and stopped just before it hit the ground.

Nothing moved in the camp for a moment. Then, a Vietnamese voice yelled into the stillness and a man with a rifle ran toward the cage.

Stone sighted the running figure with his CAR-15.

"Blow it," he told Loughlin.

The crack of his rifle came an instant before the shack blew up with a roar. The guard under Stone's rifle went down with a .223 zinger through the side of his head. The rescuers ran toward the cages. Lights all over the camp dimmed and then went out. Not a light showed. It was dark as hell.

Hog paused beside the tree. He had found the right combination of ropes and lowered the poor bastard in the tree to the ground. Then he waited for a reaction. He saw the guard running and yelling. At the same time the shack blew up, he was on his feet charging the cage he had just lowered to the ground. He found the door, broke it open, and helped the dazed and crying man from the small box.

Phil Patterson tried to stand, but he couldn't. Hog led him around in a circle for a few seconds. He was naked but he didn't seem to notice that. Hog stared at him in the soft moonlight filtering down through clouds that were scudding past.

"Can you walk, buddy?"

"Damn right." Phil grinned. "I can walk your tail off. Damn, where you guys come from? Damn, buddy, got an extra weapon? I want to kill!"

Hog gave Patterson a .45 auto, then turned and began throwing grenades. These were specials that Loughlin had souped up with C-5 plastic explosive molded around the side without the arming handle.

He pitched one at a barracks building. Men stumbled from the front door. The grenade landed on the steps, blasting four men back through the door and vaporizing the stairs. The second grenade hit the roof and blasted a hole through it as it set the thatch on fire.

Hog tugged Patterson along. They saw three riflemen dash from another building. Hog hosed them down with a dozen rounds from the CAR-15.

Patterson was shrieking at the top of his voice as he blasted with the .45. He knocked down one Viet rifleman with a shot to his head and whooped in outrageous joy.

"I've dreamed of this night for ten years!" Patterson yelled. "These bastards have been beating me and shitting on me and my buddies for years! Christ, but this is great!" He jumped in total delight.

Hog tried to angle Patterson toward the assembly point, but the big G.I. would have none of it.

"Get my buddies out! Get them out of the cages!" He turned and ran toward the cages in the center of the compound.

Hog let him go, concentrating on the barracks, which were his responsibility. He grenaded another building, leveled six of the Viet guards who had been illegally holding the Americans. They came flying out half-dressed and clawing at weapons. He shot two guards off the closest tower and turned just as a Vietnamese from inside the barracks ran through the human wreckage near the barracks door and fired a single round.

The slug took Hog high in the left arm and brought a six round burst from his CAR-15, closing the last chapter of the Viet's murderous career as a P.O.W. guard.

Hog brushed the wound with his hand. The lousy slug was still inside his shoulder. It would have to come out . . . in three or four days—didn't hardly hurt at all. Hell that dirt track crash in Atlanta had been a hell of a lot worse. He shut the bullet wound out of his mind and surged back into action.

Phil Patterson ran to the cages. He saw a big man he knew must be one of his rescuers fumbling with the locks on the cages.

"Sir, I'm a P.O.W. here; I can get the cage lock open—done it before. They are a little tricky."

Stone turned around, checked the yard, and sent a three-round burst from his Beretta 93-R at a pair of troopers storming them. Both men went down in a sprawling mass of twisted limbs and never moved again.

"I'm Stone and we're here to bust you out. What's your name?"

"Staff Sergeant Phil Patterson, Air Force. This is my buddy Corporal Doug Hillburton in this cage. The captain is in the next one. He was bad off tonight." Phil swung the door open and Hillburton came out. He was dazed, not sure what was going on.

"Buddy, it's a rescue!" Patterson shouted at him. Hillburton nodded and moved with them to the next cage.

Patterson looked through the bars and swore. He had the cage door open quickly, only to turn and shake his head.

"The captain didn't make it, sir. He's dead. He was bad off this afternoon."

"This is all of you, the three?"

"Yes, sir. We lost some last month."

"Let's get the hell out of here. Down this way, Patterson. You cover the left flank. Grab an AK when you spot one. Let's move." Stone pulled around the SPAS-12 and Patterson gaped at it.

"What in hell is that, Stone?"

"Automatic shotgun, kicks lead like a bastard. Let's haul ass."

To the left Stone saw more thatch-covered buildings taking direct hits from grenades.

They ran to the edge of the cages; then Stone swung up the shotgun and powered off two blasts. Each dropped two guards who had shed their panic and were moving toward the cages with rifles at the ready. The twenty-six lead pellets blasted them into the arms of their ancestors. Phil ran forward and grabbed one of the AK-47 rifles and three extra magazines. He grinned like a kid with a new BB gun.

On the little rise just out of the clearing, Stone saw the friendly rifles flashing their welcome covering fire.

On the left flank Loughlin had just finished with his grenades. He reached in his bag for thermite bombs and spun three of them into the blasted remains of buildings. Terrance saw them explode into flames as the intensely burning granules set fire to everything they touched.

He tossed two more, then mowed down a man who ran screaming from one of the buildings. His clothes were on fire and Loughlin gave him a mercy burst, then ran to the last building in the series.

Loughlin was aware of covering fire blasting into the building from the Cambodians. He hung back, knelt in a shadow away from the fire, and watched behind him. Stone headed for the darkness with two men in tow. Two out of three ain't bad, Loughlin decided.

Directly behind him an AK-47 stuttered and dirt flew beside Loughlin's boots. He spun, his CAR-15 up. The young Vietnamese guard who had just fired at Loughlin had a jammed rifle. He looked up at Loughlin from twenty yards, his mouth forming a scream even as the Brit's finger squeezed off a six-round burst that pulped the young soldier's chest and heart and ended his guard duty.

Loughlin ran back toward the cages to provide rear guard

fire for Stone and his M.I.A.'s when a fresh set of troopers burst from a trail beside a hut.

Loughlin dived beside the cages, pumped in a new magazine, and took out the first two fresh troops before they scattered and hit the dirt.

Nothing moved for ten seconds. Then, Loughlin found another special grenade in his pocket, pulled the pin, and overhanded the small bomb into the spot he last saw the troops.

After four seconds the grenade detonated, blasting three bodies into the air and bringing screams from the wounded. Loughlin found one more thermite grenade in his sack and he threw it into the same area. The troops there screeched in agony as the granules of raw fire ate through their clothes and flesh in an instant. Two died when splatters hit their chests and burned holes through their hearts.

Loughlin rose and ran after the moving Stone. But now there was only one man with the leader. Where in hell had the other M.I.A. got to?

Stone grabbed the back of Hillburton's tattered shirt and propelled him forward. They had to get out of the light of the burning buildings, out of the firing zone. Hillburton ran but not with convincing power. Slowly they got beyond the light and Stone pulled him down behind the first large teak tree.

"Hillburton, you stay right here. Do you understand? We're on your side. I've got to go back and help mop up. Stay here until we come to get you."

The G.I. frowned, blinked in the half light, and at last nodded.

"Stay here—stay right here—yes, sir," Hillburton said in a monotone.

Stone turned and ran back into the firelight. He had to find the other live one, Patterson. Where had he gone? In a flash of remembering what it was like to be a P.O.W., he knew what the just released man would do. Patterson would try to find a guard or maybe the camp commander to settle old debts. It could be a deadly way to try to finish an escape. Stone rushed forward, shouting Patterson's name.

Lieutenant Chau Tran huddled on the floor in the far side of his room behind an old table he had tipped on its side. This couldn't be happening! The U.S. as much as admitted there were no more P.O.W.'s. Why would they send in a rescue force?

No, it was only some freebooter, but one who was deadly. He had charged out of his door only to be hurled back inside by a rifle round in the shoulder. The Americans seemed to be everywhere. Most of the buildings were burning. The P.O.W.'s were gone by now, he was sure.

He was so close! Patterson was weakening, his mental attitude was close to where Tran wanted it! Just another two weeks with daily temptations and Patterson would have signed the letter and Chau Tran would have been paid a million dollars!

His shoulder hurt like fire. It was the first time he had ever been shot. Blood ran down the inside of his shirt. For a moment he thought of the Americans who had died in the camp. They had called him bloody bastard. Now, he was really bloody!

If he stayed quiet and slid out the escape door in the back, they would not find him. Surely they would burn this hut as well. Why did they save it to last? He frowned. The pain came back and he groaned softly.

Patterson was so close to signing the letter!

Then, he could have slipped out of Cambodia with his prisoner, got the money in Bangkok, and lived there in peace and luxury for the rest of his life. Or he could have gone to Hong Kong!

He held a small automatic in his hand. He had not fired it in weeks. He hit the ejector button and the magazine fell into his hand. With a sick feeling he knew the magazine was not loaded. He checked the chamber by feel. There was not a round there. He had no weapon!

He had to live! He had to escape and get away. By losing prisoners his future was finished in the army. He would strip off his rank and flee for Thailand. He spoke their language well. He had saved money, even though his million had not come through.

For the past six years he had nearly thirty prisoners in the camp. Some had been Khmer Rouge, others Cambodian loyalists. He had received rations and allowances from the army to care and feed the men.

A smart commander learns ways to save. Everytime a prisoner died and was not reported, it left that much rations money that Tran could keep for himself. Going from thirty prisoners to three was not the best mark as a P.O.W. specialist, but being paid for thirty gave him a good income. He could get to the border and across with no trouble, then still have enough money . . .

He sat up straighter, the pain in his shoulder forgotten. Had there been a noise outside? He moved toward the trap door that would drop him two feet to the ground. He would be gone before anyone . . .

Another spasm of a dozen rifle rounds ripped through the hut, smashing through the thin sides. One slug caught him on the right ankle and he groaned in pain. The ankle was broken! There was no way he could run for the border now! He tried to crawl to the far side of the room where his two knives lay. He had just sharpened them and cleaned the blood from the smaller one.

Again, something outside. Someone outside!

He shivered with the pain. He had never been a strong-willed man. Even as he grew up in the army, he had to force himself to be harsh. Gradually it grew into his soul as a way of life. But now, there was no chance that he would struggle out of his safety to lead his troops against the raiders. How many troops had hit him? A dozen, maybe fifteen? Part Americans, others anti-Communist guerrillas? Perhaps even some Khmer Rouge?

For a moment he was back in Hanoi with his wife and two children. His family would be well taken care of. His wife was the daughter of a high-ranking army general. He had married well. She was loving and, while not beautiful, had many good qualities. She had taught him all sexual intercourse positions. That was during the month before they were married. He had never been so exhausted in his life!

Another rifle round came through the thin walls of the hut. He shivered. Surely there would be a way out. They would grab the Americans who could walk and leave quickly. He could recoup something. He would report a company of U.S. Marines attacked him and took the prisoners and killed most of his men. He would kill any who questioned his story! Yes!

Chau Tran was feeling better. He was going to make it through this attack.

"Patterson!" Stone bellowed into the darkness. "Let's get the hell out of here. Leave the rest of the guards. Let's haul ass, Patterson!"

A burst of AK hot lead answered him. The rounds punctured the jungle clearing to his left. He darted behind the cages and checked the landscape.

Every thatched building on the place but one was burning. He could see more than a dozen bodies on the ground around the battle scene. Where the hell was Patterson?

Staff Sergeant Phil Patterson pasted himself against the back wall of the big hut Tran used. It had not been fired yet. He was not sure if the little man with the swagger stick and the sharp knife that had drawn so much blood was inside or not. Patterson still had an AK-47 and three extra magazines of ammo. But they would do no good without the evil little man.

Phil worked around to the front of Tran's hut and dived through the door. The fires did not light up the inside of the room. It was gloomy, dark. Phil heard someone breathing and pounded out an eight-round burst of automatic fire toward the sound.

When the pounding sound of the shots faded, a groan and pleading in Vietnamese scuttered through the darkness.

"A light," Patterson said in Vietnamese. "Light a candle."

He waited, a match scratched, flamed into a bright light in the small room, then a candle flickered and brightened.

Patterson stared at the half-dressed, pathetic, little self-appointed dictator. Tran shook as he looked at Patterson. His left hand showed the bloody passage of a rifle round, and he had a wound in his shoulder. "Good," Patterson muttered grimly.

"I meant no harm." Tran shouted suddenly in Vietnamese.

Patterson shot him in the left kneecap.

The Vietnamese commander shrilled a scream of agony; tears streamed down his cheeks.

"Suffer you bloody, murdering bastard!" Patterson screamed. "I know twenty-three American buddies you killed. It meant more graft you could keep for yourself, right? I should chop both your legs off and force you to beg for a living for the rest of your life. Death is too easy a sentence for you."

He lifted the rifle and fired a round into the man's genitals—then a second one.

Tran rolled in pain on the floor, his hands cradling what was left of his manhood.

"You let Captain Carlson die tonight, you scum! Now, I tell you one last time; I'll never sign your fucking ransom letter to spring me. I'm going home tonight, and you're going to die slowly, you bloody bastard!"

Tran lifted one hand pleading for mercy. He quavered, moaning on the floor of the hut. "I tried to get you home. It was all arranged. You could have been home years ago. Just by signing your name!"

"And you would have lived in luxury in China or Bangkok. No thanks. That would have killed me!"

Patterson lifted the AK-47 and slammed a round through the commander's elbow.

The Vietnamese tried to scream, but he couldn't. He looked up at Patterson; then he passed out. Patterson shot him twice in the head, edged out of the door, saw no organized resistance, and heard Stone screeching his name.

"Yeah, Stone, over here. I just had a little bit of garbage removal work to do. I'm ready to go home now."

Patterson trotted to where Stone crouched in the flickering firelight. Then the two ran back to the darkness and the tree where Hillburton waited.

"It won't be long now, guys," Stone growled. "We're going to take a nice easy walk, and then in a few hours, you'll be in Bangkok in the biggest bathtub you ever saw!"

"I could do with that!" Patterson grunted.

Hillburton blinked, not sure what had been said.

Patterson put his arms around Hillburton and closed his eyes. "I'm gonna live through today and, damn it, live through tonight! Please God, let somebody know about my plight." He looked up at Stone, then at the sky. "Thank you God, thank you!"

Chapter Five

The small Cambodian woman lay behind the AK-47 and picked her targets carefully. She did not want to harm any of the Americans. At first it was easy; she fired into every hut where men were moving. But as the battle progressed she had to be sure that the man in her sights was a Vietnamese.

She followed a green-clad Viet soldier from the barracks building on the left. He fired at the cages. She sighted, and when he stopped to fire again, she blew him away with a shot to his head. She patted the rifle, grinned, and searched for another target.

Three men burst from the jungle in back of the huts. She put a burst of six rounds into them, saw two fall, and tracked the third one who dived to the ground. She drilled three more rounds into him and saw him jolt as the rounds hit home.

The burning buildings helped her spot the enemy. Two more came from a blazing hut. She killed one before he could get his rifle up. The second one vanished into the darkness.

The woman's name was Sen; she told them that was the only name she used now. She watched her Cambodian friend firing into the burning buildings. A sharp warning from her cautioned him to be sure to hit only the enemy. He grinned and went back to work.

Sen smiled. The Americans were generous. She would earn enough for this one trip to keep her family in shelter, food, and clothes for three months. Perhaps by then she could return to her home in Cambodia. Tears stung her eyes. She knew she was dreaming. The Vietnamese would never leave Cambodia until they were driven out. Their puppet Cambodian government would help see to that.

Sen scowled and shot another Viet regular who tried to burst from the rear of a shack and run into the jungle. She pushed a new magazine in and watched for more targets to kill. Each man who fell became a monument to her dear, dead husband. The Viets had butchered him after they captured him four years ago. They used him as a human victim for knife classes.

A big man hurried from the cages. He waved an AK-47 in his hands, firing it wildly and screaming. She giggled. In the firelight she saw that the man was stark naked! He had to be an American, one of the P.O.W.'s. He must have been left that way as punishment. She fired in the same direction he did, then waited. She must not harm any of the freed men! That would be tragic.

Lon Poi, another of the Cambodian guerrillas in Stone's force, lay near Sen, three empty CAR-15 magazines beside his hot rifle. He had strict instructions to stay out of the camp, so he would not be confused with the Vietnamese. There was not always time in a combat situation to ascertain a target's nationality before firing.

He had concentrated on the left side of the camp, the barracks and two more buildings. Six men had died at his hand.

He blasted three rounds at the door of one of the huts that was not burning yet. Two more men ran out and he killed one of them.

Lon sighted a wildly running figure, but realized the man was much too large to be a Viet. Then he saw the man was naked. He would be one of the prisoners. Lon moved his sights to another hut and waited. Two men slid out through a glassless window. He caught the second one as he bellied over the bamboo. By the time he hit the ground he was dead.

Doug Hillburton shook his head again. Damn, all the shooting! It was just like when he was captured. But this time the Americans were shooting, too! Now, he understood. They were being rescued. That big guy with the black hair and ugly short shotgun had come to take him, the captain, and Phil out of there, take them home!

He cradled the AK-47 automatic rifle someone had given him. He should shoot the bastards! Yes! The bastard guards who had terrified him for ten years. He owed them!

Hillburton stood up, weaved a moment, then charged a round into the chamber and walked toward the camp. His first steps were unsteady, but then he picked up the rhythm of it. He remembered his basic training. Fire and move, fire and move.

Hillburton ran toward the camp and stopped just outside of the firelight. He went down into a prone position and watched for gooks. Where were the little bastards now that he had a way to pay them back?

A Viet rushed screaming out of a burning building. His clothes were burning. He came straight at Hillburton who lifted the rifle and pounded six slugs into the figure. The Vietnamese ran another three steps and fell just in front of Hillburton. The soldier stared at the big American; then his eyes went wide and bright and he died.

The American jumped up and ran toward the cages. Did they get everyone out? What about the captain, the skipper? How was he? He had been hurting yesterday after the beating.

Hillburton stumbled over two bodies near the cages, saw they were Vietnamese, and continued. He saw that Phil's cage was empty. Good. What about Captain Carlson? He moved toward his cage.

"Captain! Come on! Time to go home!"

He touched the captain's arm. Then, he realized the cage door was hanging open, but the skipper had not moved.

"Oh, God, no!" Hillburton screamed. He rolled him over and saw the dried blood on his throat. The gash crossed the right side of his neck. That big artery!

"Damn it, just one more fucking night, and you would have been free!"

He ran away from the cages toward the barracks. He'd find some Viets and brain them! He'd shoot their balls off and watch them scream in terror and agony. He'd kill every fucking one he could find!

The barracks on this side blazed with amazing heat. The roof had burned off and the fiery skeleton of the bamboo poles would soon collapse. No gooks in there. He turned and saw that most of the other shacks and buildings were blazing, too. A man edged round the not yet burning corner of the storage shack. Hillburton made sure it was a Vietnamese; then he slammed six rounds into him and watched him die.

He ran to the next hut. It burned fiercely. Twenty feet from it, he heard a man groan. Hillburton moved forward slowly, his finger on the trigger.

"Damn slope!" he screamed. The man's right arm had been blown off at the elbow. Blood smeared the dark ground. His face turned to Hillburton, eyes begging for help.

The American's finger tightened on the trigger. He aimed

the Russian rifle at the hated Vietnamese guard and began to squeeze the trigger.

Slowly, he shook his head. His finger eased off and he sat beside the man and put his head in his lap. The man was talking, mumbling in Vietnamese, his eyes opening and closing rapidly. His breath came in gasps.

"Buddy, you ain't gonna die alone. Damn, nobody should have to die alone. One thing I learned over here!"

The Viet looked at Hillburton as he spoke; then his eyes rolled up in their sockets and a long last gush of breath came from the soldier's collapsing lungs.

Tears seeped from Hillburton's eyes as he lay the dead man's head on the ground.

"Damn it!" Hillburton said. "What the hell is going on here?"

"Hillburton!" He heard his name called three times, grabbed his rifle, and ran back to the tree where the big guy called Stone had left him. He shook his head. What a slaughterhouse! What a fucking mess! The slopes were gonna be mad as hell come morning. Every prisoner in the place was going to have to pay for this, Hillburton suspected, once again assuming his prisoner status. Who was yelling at him? And in English. They probably wouldn't get fed at all tomorrow. Christ, they would all really be hurt for this fire!

Punishment. Yeah, punishment. But he could take it. He could take it for as long as they dished it out. Someday, somebody would come. Yeah, he could take it. Hillburton was tough stock. Damn tough stock. He could take it. Yeah. He could take it.

He ran up to the tree and sat down beside it. The guy called Stone grinned and whacked him on the back.

"Hey, buddy, thought we lost you. We're about ready to pull out of this shit-hole."

Hillburton nodded. He could take anything they could

dish out. Hell, yes! Do what they told you, don't sass them, and eat everything they gave you and everything you could steal. Damn, he was going to hang on and eventually get out of this damn Cambodian Hilton!

Mark Stone frowned as he knelt beside Hillburton. The man was in a world all his own. For some reason he could not accept the idea that he was a free man, that he was being rescued from the Viets. In time, maybe in time, he would snap out of it. Maybe, but Stone would not give you odds one way or the other.

Hog Wiley threw his last grenade at six guards who rushed him. The *zinging* shrapnel cut down two of them. His CAR-15 nailed the third one, and then the last one was on him, a knife out front searching for vital organs. Hog slapped away the blade, grabbed the man in a bear hug, turned, and fell on top of the small attacker, slamming the wind out of his lungs.

Hog was up in a flash, his heavy boots coming down on the Vietnamese's head in a crushing stomp. A second kick on the side of the head broke the soldier's neck and he lay with dead eyes staring at his burning barracks.

The big, ugly, hairy Texan moved into shadows and searched his sector. He could find no living enemy. Drag-ass time. He retreated in plotted rushes. Clearing the area in front and behind each time, taking no chances on being surprised on either side. He caught one more camp guard running for the safety of the darkness and blew his head apart with two rounds.

Then, he was back at the point of departure.

Stone came up a moment later, followed by one of the M.I.A.'s.

"How many we get?"

"Two. Hillburton here and Patterson. A captain was dead in his cage. Checked out earlier tonight," Stone replied.

"Damn close."

Hog looked at Hillburton. "This guy don't look none too good."

"He should snap out of it, but it may take some time."

"Gonna be harder."

"Move back to the support fire position on that little rise with Hillburton. Rest of us are coming soon." Stone looked at Hog. "You all right, Wiley? You're carrying your left arm funny."

"Picked up some stray lead. No sweat."

"We'll check it out before we move far. Now get going."

Stone went back into the firelight looking for Patterson. He saw him come out of the only shack not burning. He grabbed a half-burned length of bamboo and threw the blazing stick on the shack's roof. The thatch blazed up in a few seconds and Patterson screamed with laughter and danced away.

"Patterson! Patterson, over here on the double!" Stone called into the night.

Patterson stepped from behind a tree not ten feet from Stone and grinned. "You want me, Captain?" he said.

"Make it sargeant, and yes, I want you. Time to get ourselves out of this snake pit. Also time to find you a pair of pants to fit you. Hog's most likely."

Loughlin ran from the light into the darkness, a single rifle shot chasing him. He slid, panting, to the ground near Stone and the M.I.A.

"I kicked ass on that last batch. I think we got ourselves out of here free and clear."

"No casualties?"

"None I know of," the Brit said. "We got us two free Americans, ex-P.O.W.'s and no spare lead. Time to haul it."

They moved back toward the support fire rise where Sen and the other three Cambodians along with Hog and Hillburton waited. Stone asked Hog if he brought an extra pair of pants. He did and they fit Patterson but were a bit short.

When Patterson put on a brand new white T-shirt, he almost cried.

The Cambodians still watched the camp and fired a shot now and then to keep the survivors' heads down and let them know they could not move anywhere.

Loughlin picked a narrow spot in the trail and rigged two trip wires for grenades. He left them on hair trigger release, and the little band marched away up the trail, back toward their LZ.

Stone checked his watch. It was just after 0030 hours. They had six hours to hike back to the landing zone.

Stone took one last look at the burning camp.

"We haven't heard the last of those guys," he growled. "Phil said he wasted the camp commander. One of his ambitious underlings will gather up the fighting men he has left and take a swing at us. The faster we get down this trail the better."

Chapter Six

Stone set up the order of march with a practiced hand. He led off and set Hog in the rear. In between he put Sen, the Cambodian woman right behind him, then came Patterson, and a Cambodian man, then Hillburton. He assigned Loughlin to baby-sit Hillburton.

"He goes a little wiggy sometimes, Terrance, so watch him. Stay behind him and keep your eyes peeled. He might be fine, I'm not sure. You better carry the AK-47 he has that we borrowed from the Viets."

Loughlin grinned and bobbed his head. "Anybody coming out of that place would have his had screwed on just a little crazy. I'll tuck him in and everything. Don't worry your bones about him, mate."

The line of march continued with the other two Cambodians and Hog in the rear.

Stone set a blistering pace the first hour. They heard the grenades go off far behind them when the trap sprung. It could be enough to discourage the camp guards from any more pursuit.

When Stone figured they were halfway to the LZ, he opened his pack and took out the small walkie-talkie and punched up the send button.

"Dragonfly. Calling Dragonfly. This is Creeper. Over."

There was only the silent air pounding back at them. Stone made the call twice more, waited a half hour, and made it again.

This time the speaker crackled and then settled down.

"Yes, Creeper. Dragonfly here ready to move. Do you have an ETA?"

"That's a positive, big buddy. Make it as arranged. I say again, our meet should be at the time already set up."

"Loud and clear here, Creeper. As arranged. We have noticed a patrol in the area so be alert. See you then."

Patterson was fading. After his first euphoric hyperactivity upon release, he calmed down, and as they marched, he began to weave and wander along the trail.

Sen warned Stone about the big American. He had been bumping into her or dragging back twenty yards. She had taken his Russian rifle, but still he was slow and unsteady.

Stone called a halt to let everyone rest. He dropped down beside Patterson.

"How's it going, Sergeant?"

"Damn great! Just fantastic! This is the most beautiful day of my whole damn life!"

"But you're getting a little wiped out, right?"

"Yeah, but it still feels good!"

Stone gave Phil two thick, chocolate bars. They had melted once already, but now were solid in the cooler night air.

"Eat both of these, right now. They probably will give you diarrhea tomorrow, but the energy is what you need now. You're just sapped of all your strength. Don't be afraid to yell if I'm moving too fast."

"Hell, man, I'm doing great! I can keep up. I haven't

felt better in ten years! I'm free, man! You know what the hell that feels like!"

"Yes, Phil I do. I spent some time in a Viet prison camp myself. Now, rest up a couple more minutes."

He brought the Cambodian woman back to Hog at the end of the line.

"Let's take a look at that shoulder." He had told the woman one of the men was wounded.

Hog pushed his T-shirt sleeve up and they saw the ugly gash even through the nighttime gloom.

"Bad," Sen said.

She looked at the supplies in the small first aid kit Stone took out of his pack.

Sen probed a moment and Hog flinched.

"Didn't hurt none; just flicked my bic in there," Hog said trying to sound cool.

"Too deep," Sen said. "He pass out, pow! I try to get it now. Later, more better time." She put disinfectant on the wound, then some ointment, then a compress, and wrapped the whole thing with an inch-wide bandage and taped it securely.

"Keep plenty safe to Thailand," she said.

"Great gobs of goose shit!" Hog said. "She's a woman! Why the hell we bring a damn woman? She's a Cambode guerrilla? Hell, I thought we learned our lesson with that Jackie Winslow broad. Now, we have a woman shooter?"

"I didn't know she was a woman when we left. She's probably a better shot than any of us. Besides, she's got a score to settle with the Viets. And she speaks English. The bastard Viets killed her husband slow and hard, I'd guess. Too late for objections now. She was the one with the machete who separated that Viet from his head back at the silent hit. You remember that, Hog. You went to help her."

"Christ! That was her?" He lifted his eyebrows. Then he shrugged. "Hell, looks like she can do the job."

"She can. You okay on this end?"

"Course, why not? Just a little gouge out of my arm. I still got two good ones left!" Hog laughed and Sen didn't understand, which was fine with Stone.

He and Sen went back to the head of the column. On their way they passed Patterson who was pumping Loughlin about everything.

"What do you mean, you don't know where the Dodgers finished in the pennant race last year? Were they in the series?"

Loughlin went around that one and told him about rock-and-roll. He had to go back a long way before he found a group that Patterson knew besides the Beatles.

Stone checked his watch. The ten minutes were up.

"Saddle up," Stone said. "Let's move out. We've got a bus to catch."

A half mile up a long slippery path toward the top of a small hill, Sen pulled on Stone's sleeve. She pointed to her ear and then ahead.

Stone held up his hand and the line of march stopped, everyone dropping to one knee, weapons ready, safeties off.

Stone listened closely, and he heard the sound of boots moving toward them on the soft trail ahead.

Stone waved everyone off the trail and into the dense growth that was still wet. They crouched behind betel palm and a few pines on this higher hill and waited.

Three minutes later a ten-man Cambodian regular army patrol came swinging along the jungle trail. The troopers looked young, but Stone could never tell the age of an Oriental. Everyone held silent as the group went past. They waited another five minutes, then got back on the trail.

Stone checked his watch. They had a long way to go yet. It would be much quicker if they did not run into more patrols.

A half hour later they slipped through the same dead

quiet village they had on their way in. There was no one there but the chickens and the sleeping people. Stone breathed a small sigh of thanks when they were back in the jungle, marching along the trail.

It rained again. Stone could not remember the number of quick, hard showers they had experienced since they left the chopper. The wetness crept into every dry spot he had left and he laughed softly. It would make that hot shower tonight in Bangkok seem all the sweeter.

It was like playing football in the rain. The first few tackles on the muddy field were strange. Then, after you and everyone else was wet through, a little more mud, mire, and rain didn't mean a thing.

Time dragged. Stone kept looking at his watch, punching the little light so he could be sure.

Oh-three-forty-five hours.

Patterson was making do. He limped now on his left leg, but he was grinning. Stone decided the guy would get there if he had to crawl.

Oh-four-thirty hours.

Doug Hillburton was feeling better. He was back in the present for a few miles, laughing and joking about getting away from the slopes.

Stone had put Sen in the lead. She was a better point man than he was. She could hear things he failed to. She moved ahead at his pace and the time slid by.

Paterson kept pumping Loughlin.

"So who is the big-titted blond bombshell in Hollywood?" he asked. "The new Marilyn Monroe?"

"There just isn't one, Patterson. The contract studio system was gone before you shipped over. No big-chested blonde has really made it like Marilyn. Oh, there's Dolly Parton; she claims a pair of forty-two inchers, but nobody I know has measured them. She sings mostly."

"Forty-two inches . . . tits? Wow—wow—wow! She can

sing for me anytime, I don't care what she sounds like."

"Millions of men feel the same way you do, Patterson. They just can't feel far enough to reach those beauties. But they sure as hell keep trying."

Oh-six hundred hours. They were at the LZ a half hour before the contact time. Good!

Stone looked across a small stream at the spot where the chopper was supposed to be. At first he couldn't find it; then through some oddly positioned palm tree branches, he saw the bird.

Stone took out his radio, punched it on, then spoke. "Dragonfly, the Creeper is close by."

"Creeper you are five by five. Visual?"

"Amen and hallelujah, ready to walk on the water."

"We'll clear and get the engines warm. Out."

Stone waved to the team. "Everything is A-OK. The chopper is here. Why don't we get across the stream down there and catch the last bus for Bangkok?"

There was a small cheer, and the column moved down the rise to the edge of the river.

Just then, all hell broke loose.

Rifle fire hit the chopper, followed by the *whoosh* of what could only be some kind of rocket. Even a near miss on the chopper by a rocket round could change their transportation plans for getting home.

"Back to the trees!" Stone shouted, and they raced the thirty yards into the brush and jungle before any rifle shots came at them. The enemy strategy was clear. Kill the horse and nobody could ride her home.

From behind a towering teak tree, he watched the drama unfold. Nobody was shooting at his team. Rifle fire from three hundred yards away had driven the chopper crew to cover. The first *whoosh*ing rocket missed the bird by twenty yards. Where were the riflemen shooting from?

At once, a second shoulder-fired rocket of some kind

lanced from the same position the riflemen were using.

"Fire up there—where the rifles are!" Stone shouted. Nine rifles joined in the counterattack, pouring a barrage into a slight rise.

Just then the rocket round hit the chopper dead on the Plexiglas windshield and exploded. A moment later the fuel tanks went and the chopper was one huge ball of fire as a black cloud rose slowly in the early morning. Nobody near the chopper could have lived.

"Let's get them!" Stone shouted, and they began an orderly charge through the dense jungle, moving from cover to cover, circling the edge of the clearing, and heading for the place from which the attack had been launched.

Patterson ran ahead; Stone threatened to shoot him if he didn't stay with the squad. He pointed out that it was dangerous to be in front of advancing, friendly troops.

"Air Force types don't get infantry training, Sarge," he called, "but we try harder."

By the time they had moved two hundred yards, they saw that the squad of Viet regulars had dug into a forward slope and had taken only one casualty from the original firing. They were sassy and dumped a ton of rifle rounds at Stone's men as soon as the two forces were in contact.

Stone told Hog to keep the team firing, to lay down covering rounds, as Loughlin and he took a swing around to their flank. Stone still had the automatic shotgun slung over his back. The tube was filled with eight rounds, all deadly double-ought buckshot.

"Search and sucker?" Loughlin asked.

"Yeah, whoever gets to the best position. We have more of those grenades?"

"Running low, but every man has two of them. Check in your pack."

Stone dug them out and clipped them to his pack straps. They moved, running silently and quickly through the rotting, damp, infested jungle.

Loughlin was ahead. He stopped suddenly, his hand unsheathing a six-inch knife from his right hip. He jumped sideways, then slashed out with the blade, swung back the other way, and then whistled the weapon through the air again. The head of a snake fell to a log, minus its body.

"Yeah!" he said softly. "Little old kraik about six feet long wanted to use this log all private like. Never did like a damn pushy snake."

They moved again, turned right, and now made sure they did not disturb a leaf or soggy stick as they slid through the jungle stew toward the clearing. Near the water the jungle seemed damper and boglike.

Loughlin spotted them first. He signaled and moved up cautiously, clearing a path, avoiding trees, and trying for a good open space where he could throw a grenade without hitting the overhanging trees.

Stone had moved just as quietly up a line thirty feet from Loughlin. Both were sweating despite the morning coolness. Stone saw that Loughlin had found his spot. He was twenty yards from the Viets ahead. There were six to eight of them dug in, taking occasional fire from Hog and his people, but the rounds were not effective against the men who were well hidden in their foxholes.

Loughlin raised his hand. He was ready. Stone gave him an advance sign with his hand and the Britisher pitched a grenade. It sailed free for ten yards, then hit the branch of a hardwood tree, and dropped. Before it hit the ground, Loughlin had thrown a second.

The first grenade, which fell short, went off with a deadly roar. The targets jumped up and looked behind them. They were totally exposed when the second grenade landed in their midst and exploded with a cracking blast that made Stone's ears ring.

Stone lifted up and peppered the survivors with four

spaced rounds from his shotgun, watching the .32 caliber slugs rip into anything in their way, especially young Vietnamese bodies. Stone loved the combat shotgun! He was going to take it on as many missions as possible.

Stone dropped down and waited. There was no response from the Viets. He lifted again; a rifle cracked from ahead. On top of the sound came the six-round stutter of a CAR-15 and the Viet screamed and fell halfway out of his hole, his back sprayed with hot, angry lead.

Loughlin moved up this time, until he had a visual on the position.

"Looks like a bingo, Sarge," he said.

"Any numbers missing?"

"Can't be sure..."

A chattering CAR-15 drowned out his last words; then all was quiet in the jungle.

"I'd say now we have our bingo," Loughlin said.

That was when they both looked back toward the men they had left. A heavy concentration of rifle fire from somewhere behind their main body turned the morning into a second battlefield that could get bloody in a rush.

Loughlin and Stone reloaded as they ran back the way they had come. The ambushers had set up a second force as a surprise. It must not have been in position when the visitors arrived. This was not the kind of surprise that let mercenaries live to a ripe old age.

Chapter Seven

Stone and Loughlin found plenty of cover to protect themselves on the way to the rest of their team. They slid into position behind a huge teak log and Hog bellowed at them.

"Sons of bitches sneaked in behind us. We lost one of the Cambodians, the guy called Lon, I think. He was hit awful bad. No way to save the little guy. Patterson got grazed on his butt. He'll live. I think the little woman is hit, too, but she won't let me check."

"We need to get a team down to the chopper—see if the pilot is still in one chunk," Stone said.

Hog shook his head.

"Not a chance. He got caught in the exploding aviation fuel. I saw him get it. Now much left of him but a crispy critter by now."

Stone scowled. It was a term he hadn't heard in years. They used it in 'Nam to refer to the remains of troops or civilians caught in a napalm drop and burned into unrecognizable chunks of ash and bone.

Another volley of buzzing rounds slammed into the trees and around and over the log.

"How many out there, you figure?" Loughlin asked.

"Eight or ten," Hog said.

Sen had crawled up to the trio.

"Eight Viets," she said, "I count."

Stone grinned. "Hog, is she earning her keep?"

"Damn right," he blustered, "always said she would."

Loughlin screwed up his face.

"She? Sen is a woman?"

"For twenty-five to thirty years, I'd guess," Stone said. "Now, let's get rid of the riffraff out there and decide what we're going to do. We've got ourselves one hell of a big problem with no transport. It's more than a two-hundred mile walk back to Thai country, and that's through about one hundred sixty thousand Viet troops and a whole shit-pot full of Cambodian regulars."

"My turn," Hog said. "I'll take Patterson and blast this last bunch—cut them off on the figure-eight track. Patterson's gung ho for some more action."

"Not Patterson. We're not going to lose him in a lousy little firefight now. Use one of the guerrillas."

"Me go," Sen said. She checked her AK-47 and showed them four more filled magazines and the pair of grenades. They were the Russian style and damn effective.

"Fine by me," Hog said. "She can understand me. We'll do the great circle tour."

"We'll keep their heads down," Patterson said, crawling up to the group. He scowled at Stone. "I hear you outrank me, Master Sergeant Stone. Only damn problem is, I'm active duty, and you're a wild-eyed civilian." He chuckled. "But I'm under your command. Course I also damn well know you're right. But I want to pull my weight.

"Hell, so we have to walk two hundred and forty miles. At twenty miles a day we'll be there in only twelve days!

I can do that standing on my head and walking on my hands! Look what the hell I been doing for the past years!"

Patterson stopped and looked at them. "Hey, what is the exact date? What *year* is this?"

"February 16, 1986," Stone told him.

Patterson stared at him. "No shit? We were shot down in 1973! Thirteen fucking years!" Patterson turned away and brushed at angry tears. Then, he lifted up and fired three rounds at the spot where the Viets were last seen and caught ten shots in return.

"Well, the bastards are still there," Stone said.

Hog and Sen had vanished into the deep green, deadly jungle to their left. They would make a sweep around and come in to the side or behind the other troops—if they were still there . . .

"Pin down those suckers!" Stone shouted. "Everyone on line. Let's keep them right where they are."

The firing pace picked up considerably.

"Don't use it all up!" Stone shouted.

One Viet figured the scam and took a flying run for the jungle wall ten yards away. The two forces were less than fifty yards from each other. Stone tracked the man and blasted him with three rounds just before the man made the cover.

Firing from the other side slackened.

"Getting short of ammo over there?" Patterson asked.

Stone shook his head. "They're just waiting to see what we're going to do. We have a lot farther to go to get home than they do. They can chase our asses for months, harass us all the way to the border."

Patterson tossed a grenade up and down in his hand.

"No way you can throw that fifty yards," Stone said. "We'll have better use for them later."

Stone glanced at his watch. It had been almost five minutes since Hog left.

"Let's hit them harder," Stone shouted. "Hog should be nearly in position."

They let loose a two-minute barrage at the logs and trees where the Viets had taken cover.

As they began to slacken their support fire, they head two grenades go off. Parts of green-clad bodies sailed through the air. Then one AK-47 and a CAR-15 out front growled and chattered and Stone called his people to cease fire.

Two minutes later it was all over. Hog waved a white flag and then stood up where the enemy troops had been.

"Dog meat," he said.

Stone told the rest of the people to stay undercover and he took off at a trot toward the chopper with Loughlin. It still smoked as the seat cushions burned. Now, it was only a hollow shell of aluminum girders and twisted plastic. Part of the Plexiglas had melted.

Stone found the Irishman face down twenty yards from the bird. He had been blown there by the fuel explosion. When Stone turned the man over he sucked in a breath. There was no face left, no throat, no chest, all burned off by the superheated flaming aviation gasoline.

They checked the bird. Everything had been destroyed, charred into ashes. There was not a thing that could be salvaged. Hog walked down and shook his head.

"Looks like we got ourselves quite a little problem here, boss man."

"Seems so. How did your side man do on your shoot-out?"

Hog grinned. "I ain't never seen a little gal shoot up a storm like she can. Bet she can take five legs off a spider one at a time from fifty yards with that AK-47. Damn, but she can make it talk! Said she had used one several times before in combat. She let me throw the grenades, and then she was whipsawing the survivors like they were pieces of wood! She did a number on anything that moved. Nerves like steel bands, she has."

"I think she passed Hog's final exam," Loughlin said. "Now, what the hell are we going to do from here on out?"

"So we scratch one chopper," Stone said. "All is not fucking lost." He reached into his pack and took out the radio. "An Khom said this thing had a range of over three hundred miles. If so, we simply tell the man we need transport and to send in another chopper."

"Simple," Hog said, "if An Khom has his set turned on this time of morning."

Mark pushed the switch on and waited a minute; then he pushed talk. "Creeper calling Big Bear, Bangkok. This is Creeper calling Big Bear, Bangkok. Come in Big Bear. Over." They waited a minute, then repeated the call twice. "For an emergency call we try every hour on the hour," Stone said.

Loughlin held out his hand. He took the radio and checked the switch. "The little on-off light doesn't come on with the switch," he said. "Sure the batteries are good?"

"They were a half hour ago."

Loughlin turned the set over and frowned. An AK-47 slug extended outward from the back of the set. The rest of it was inside in the guts of the radio.

"Now, we do have a problem," Stone said. "I must have picked that up on that last little go-round. I remember getting hit with something in the back. I thought it was a branch falling off a tree."

Loughlin looked at his pack, put the radio back, and laughed softly.

"We don't have a radio that works, but at least we have our leader. That bloody radio saved your ass, Stone. That zinger would have slashed into your tender body just about at your backbone and broken your spinal column or come out through a lung and your heart."

They all stood there in the grass beside the rivers that

made a V and stared at the radio.

Stone shook the offending bit of technology, shook it a few times more, and tried the switches again. Nothing. He tossed it on the ground near the dead chopper.

"There was some talk with An Khom about a contingency plan, but nothing was written in blood. He's a businessman and won't worry a lot when his chopper fails to return. His fee was on credit this time. Double or nothing. But he didn't figure on losing a bird. Hell, let's eat the rest of our rations and figure out what the hell to do next."

Back at the big teak log, they saw the three Cambodians clustered around the fourth.

Stone went over to check. Sen looked up.

"It is Lon; he is wounded very bad. Not move again. Does not want to be captured by Communists."

Stone sat on the damp jungle floor beside the quiet, tiny woman.

"Sen, I'm not sure what you're asking. You say he can't be moved. You know we can't stay here."

She waved her hand in front of her face.

"No, no. Just tell you. Lon tell me what to do. When we go, we leave him a pistol. Is possible?"

"Yes, but . . ."

"No, Lon Poi decide."

Stone patted her on the shoulder and gave her a .45 automatic from his pack that was fully loaded. He handed her two more loaded magazines. She shook her head and gave him back the extra magazines. Then she took the magazine from the .45 and made sure there was not a round in the chamber. She skillfully unloaded all but two rounds from the magazine and handed the extra cartridges back to Stone who took them with a puzzled frown on his face.

Sen put the magazine in the weapon and pulled the slide, charging one round into the chamber; then she pushed on the safety.

"Lon Poi thank you. I thank you. Fighters for a free Cambodia thank you."

She turned from him then and went back to where the other two Cambodians knelt near their fallen comrade.

Stone moved up where the Americans waited for him.

"Okay, you guys know the situation. We're two hundred forty miles from the closest Thai territory. We have weapons; we can appropriate plenty of ammo before we leave here and new firearms if we need them from the last firefight.

"We are short on food and supplies since we counted on a quick turnaround. We have no transport of any kind. Now I want your suggestions."

"Hell, Sarge, we walk out," Patterson said.

"Chances of doing that are damn slim," Loughlin countered.

"Just suggestions right now," Stone said. "No arguments or logic."

"Float down the Mekong," Hog said.

"Walk out," Loughlin suggested.

"Live off the land, raid villages," Patterson added.

Stone turned to Hillburton. The corporal was in another land again. He could hear and see and obey commands, but he had retreated into his private world.

Stone looked at each of them again.

"As I see it, we have three options. One, we can try to hike out of this place. We might find some ox carts along the way, but not likely. Two, we can mess up and get captured and stuffed back into another P.O.W. camp. Three, we can hole up somewhere and go down with a blazing AK in one hand and a CAR-15 in the other hand until we run out of ammo and get our asses shot off. Comments by each of you. Hog?"

"No choice—we hike."

"Really no options at all, Stone," Loughlin said. "We have to walk out or die trying."

Patterson grinned. "Shit, Sarge, no question. We got to hike our butts off. We better get moving."

Stone looked at Hillburton, then nodded. "It's unanimous. Lon Poi is wounded bad. He can't be moved. He's got a .45; that's what he wanted. We better check our weapons. We should pick up two more AK-47's if somebody wants to carry them. We will be running out of ammo for the CAR-15's soon, and we can steal all the other ammo we can find around here. We might be damn glad we have those AK-47's down the road."

"Let's take all the filled AK magazines we can find. Patterson, you use an empty pack and go up to that first firefight. Hog, you get everything you can from the second one. Grenades, too, and anything else we can carry. *Carry* is the important word here."

Ten minutes later they had divided the rations they had left and eaten them. There was nothing else; they were ready. They found a smashed radio at the first firefight. The Viets could have called in some more bodies to help.

They liberated twenty-eight filled magazines. Four men carried AK-47 rifles and four magazines. The rest of the enemy ammo went into packs.

"West," Stone said, "we need to strike almost due west to find our spot. The first big problem will be the Mekong It's probably a half mile, maybe a mile wide up here."

Stone signaled to Sen. She said something to the Cambodians. Each bent and embraced the dying man, then turned and left without looking back. Sen was the last. She put a jungle flower in Lon Poi's hand, then the .45 automatic in the other. Stone saw that she pushed the safety off, then kissed his cheek, turned, and walked away.

They were only a hundred yards down the trail when they heard the booming sound of the .45 automatic. It came just once.

Sen turned to Stone and nodded.

"Lon Poi's pain is ended. His new life will start soon. Buddha will protect him."

Stone set up the same order of march as before, putting Sen out front. They began working west toward the mighty Mekong that slashed through this broad plain like a gorging knife. He figured the river's edge was about ten miles away.

Chapter Eight

Stone was pleased with their march of the past two hours. They had put some distance between them and the burned chopper and any fresh troops the Viets might be rushing to the spot.

He slashed at an overhanging vine, clipping it in half with Sen's machete, and then snorted. He could not vent his anger at the situation on the jungle.

It was possible to cross Cambodia by foot—if they took their time, stayed in the unpopulated areas, lived off the land, and did not run into any big concentration of troops. The *if* was the rub.

The latest intel on the Vietnamese that he got before he left Bangkok was that this was the start of the three-month dry season, when the bogs and jungles and roads dried out a little. The Viets had staged dry-season offensives each of the six previous years, and they were expected to again. One source said they would bring in an extra forty thousand troops from the Chinese border to use for a search and destroy mission through the sweeping lowlands of Cambodia on both sides of the Mekong.

Stone and his crew were smack in the middle of that find and kill zone. Beside that, the Viets would have more than a dozen Russian T-54 tanks to spearhead the attacks. Soon the roads would dry enough so the tanks could operate.

As they marched, Stone kept a wary eye on his two P.O.W.'s and saw that they were making it. Hillburton seemed to be the stronger now, perhaps because he was not wasting a lot of nervous energy feeling free the way Patterson did. Both would make it—if the rest of them did.

He began to list what he needed. First, some way across the Mekong, then a guide to help them stay away from populated centers and keep them on back trails and heading west; then food. Already his belly was beginning to feel the need for some fuel. They would have to eat off the land tonight.

There were coconut palms he had seen and every so often they found a splash of banana trees. They were not your normal supermarket variety, probably an import from South China years ago, but he had seen some stalks that looked ripe and ready. What about meat and potatoes? Fighting food?

Sen signaled to him and he stopped. Her hand was up and he lifted his so the file behind him would stop and go down. Sen had a strange look on her face, something between anger and fright, he couldn't tell which.

"Very bad," she said and stared down the trail. "Strange, the little people be here. I find their sign twice, now again."

"Sen, I don't understand. What little people?"

"Aborigines, the ancient people. They have roamed these lands for centuries. It is said the only man who goes into the little people's country is a man being clawed to pieces by a tiger."

"Folklore, Sen? Superstitions?"

"Partly. But they are unfriendly, warlike, attack anyone in their area. During World War II they killed whole companies of expert Japanese troops."

"Is there a way around them?"

"Not without going back a distance. Usually they are in the mountains, where few people go. They must be down here for some ritual or for some kind of material they need."

"Why do you call them little people?"

"They are small, no more than three feet tall."

"Pygmies."

"Yes."

Stone chewed it around a minute. No way they could go back. Viets would be swarming all over that chopper by now. It was a little after 0900 hours. He motioned for her to stay in place and then went back along the line briefing the Americans.

"Play it cool; we'll try to bluff our way through if we see them. They might be afraid of us, too."

"Damn sure hope so," Patterson said. "Hate to get this far just to wind up in a pygmy stew. Most of them are cannibals, you know that, Sarge? We heard about them from time to time in camp. Wished the little rascals would come and chew on some of the fat guards we had."

Back at the point, Stone asked Sen about that. "Oh, yes, all little people eat human flesh." She winced and he saw a red stain on her green fatigue shirt pocket.

"You're hurt!"

"Just a scratch."

"Where?"

"On chest . . . on my . . . breast. Not bad."

'Let's dress it. I need you healthy and strong." He stopped the line of marchers.

She protested a moment; then he took out the first aid kit and she unbuttoned the heavy shirt and pulled up a white cotton T-shirt. One of her small breasts had a gouge in it about an inch long. It had bled a lot. He washed the blood off, then let her treat herself. He put a bandage on and wrapped it around her back to be sure it stayed in place.

"I'm sorry to embarrass you, Sen. But today you are a soldier, not a woman. That makes it safer for you, too. Back in Bangkok you can be a woman again."

She bowed. "Thank you. You fine man."

They moved a short time later. Sen's worried frown deepened.

"More sign, little footprints in mud."

They continued and were near a small stream that came bouncing down from a series of low hills when Sen stopped suddenly and pointed ahead.

A human head lay in the trail. A bamboo lance had been driven through the mouth and out the back of the neck. The face was Oriental, but Stone could not say from what country.

"It is the final warning not to enter," Sen said.

"Do these little people use guns?"

"No, primitive weapons—bows, arrows, lances."

Stone pulled his eight-inch fighting knife from the scabbard down his left leg and held it by the back side of the blade. It was made of the best steel and finely sharpened four inches back from the tip. Now and then he shaved with it.

He took the point and walked normally with the knife held sideways in front of him. Occasional shafts of sunlight breaking through the treetop canopy glinted and flashed off the bright blade.

They had gone only another hundred yards when Stone saw movement ahead. A small man wearing only a loincloth and holding a bamboo spear that had been split to form three sharpened points stood in the center of the trail. The pygmy was three feet tall and had a wisp of a beard and fierce, glaring eyes. His legs were spread, his fist on his left hip. The tiny man's whole posture one of authority.

Stone looked to his left. Three more abos stood there.

To the right was another trio and then along each side of the trail a column of twenty little men appeared. Each had a spear, and the spears were all tipped with some blood-red substsance that was not merely for decoration.

Sen eased up beside Stone. The first abo looked intently at the big knife.

The small man chattered at them. It was a language not common in the country. Stone had never heard it. He looked at Sen. She smiled and replied with a few words.

"Give him the knife" Stone said.

Sen spoke again, pointing at the knife Stone held in a manner that it could not be used as a weapon.

The small man ahead frowned and motioned to one of the men near him. The abo held his spear pointed ahead of him and skittered forward more like an animal than a man walking. He used the shaft of the spear to push the knife from Stone's hand and then threatened them both with the lance and they backed up.

The pygmy grabbed the knife by the handle and ran, chattering excitedly, to the head man.

The chief took the weapon and examined it, received a piece of bamboo on command, and sliced at it with the knife. The blade slanted through the green stalk as if it were water.

The forty voices of the surrounding pygmy men hissed in approval. It was their way of showing they liked the gift.

"Tell him the knife is a gift from a friend. All we want is safe passage to the river."

Sen struggled getting the words out. At last she had made the chief understand. He smiled, swung the knife, and cut vines and small bamboo, grinning at this new toy.

Then one of the men touched him and whispered. The abos faded into the jungle.

Sen shook her head. "Don't move, anyone. Something has alerted them."

Stone passed the word down the line. "Freeze—stay in place. The little guys are either scared of something or setting a trap. Freeze but be ready. No firing without my command. But I don't think we should use our weapons."

Ahead, Stone heard it—something was coming, a patrol, maybe a company, soldiers. Soon they could hear laughing and voices. The five-man Vietnamese regular army patrol came around a bend in the trail and stopped.

The point man yelped in Vietnamese to the man behind him. A Viet with stripes on his sleeve moved forward, his AK-47 up and ready.

"Who are you?" he asked them in Vietnamese, leveling his rifle at them. He was twenty yards from Sen.

"Little people are all around us," Sen said. "The pygmy cannibals."

The leader of the patrol laughed.

"You must be a coward or an old woman to believe those wild stories of ancient, toothless men in the hills. Show me one of them!"

Just then an abo appeared ten feet from him.

The soldier moved his rifle and fired six rounds, but the abo had anticipated the attack and jumped to safety behind a teak tree.

Before any of the others could fire, twenty poison-tipped bamboo spears lanced through the morning Cambodian ambiance and impaled the five Viet soldiers.

No more shorts were fired. The abos yelled, then rushed forward, slashed the throats of the men, and recovered their spears. After more jabbering and hand waving, a dozen small women came in and stared at the strangers. They wore long skirts and their breasts and torsos were covered by brightly colored cloth. The chief shouted a command, perhaps a warning, and two women grabbed each Viet by the feet and dragged the bodies into the jungle.

The leader of the pygmies came out again and this time

walked to within ten feet of Sen and Stone. He talked slowly
and gave Sen time to translate to Stone.

"He says we are kind to make a gift to him. He is glad
that we did not use our bang-bangs. Everyone who uses a
bang-bang must die. Now, he invites us to a marvelous feast.
All the native fruits of the jungle, a delicious snake dish,
and the fattest of the Viets just killed will be . . . will be
roasted for our pleasure."

Sen's eyes went wide as she said the last words.

Stone grinned. "Tell him we thank him, that we are from
a land far across the sea, and must hurry to the big river.
We would like to give him a second present." Slowly Stone
reached for his right boot, unsnapped a sheat, and drew out
a four-inch knife. He held it by the steel, the handle toward
the chief.

An abo jumped toward him, pushed out his spear, and
tapped Stone's wrist lightly. Stone dropped the knife so it
stuck in the trail, and the abos hissed in delight.

The point man picked up the knife and, holding it by the
blade as Stone had, handed it to his chief.

Sen gave him Stone's message and he smiled, then danced
around in a circle.

"He's delighted," Sen said. "Knives are the most important item one of these men can own. Now, he has two
new ones in one day!"

"Hope he doesn't get over enthusiastic and want to marry
me," Stone said.

The chief calmed down and chattered to one of his go-
fers and the man sprinted into the jungle.

The chief looked at Sen. He talked and she translated.

"The leader says we all are free to go. You understand
good manners as some do not. He will treasure his gifts.
He wishes we could stay for the victory dance and the
celebration and feast, but he, too, has been far from home."

As she finished translating, two women came in carrying

large baskets of fruit. Many of the fruits Stone had never seen. The chief said a few more words, then the forty abos vanished into the jungle in less than two seconds, and Stone and his party were alone, wondering how the small men of the forest and jungle could vanish so completely and so quickly.

Sen checked the fruit and said it was all edible, and they each carried three or four pieces, leaving the trays near the trail where the women would return for them.

They moved more rapidly then, and a half mile farther on, Sen said she no longer found the small footprints of the pygmies. They relaxed a little, and Stone figured they had another two or three miles to go to get to the river.

Sen told Stone that the little people wander in Vietnam, Cambodia, Laos, and Thailand. They have no concept of nations or borders, speak a strange dialect of Vietnamese, and go happily on their nomadic ways, chomping on game from the forests and jungles or on a tender human roast whenever one falls into their hands, such as today.

She said they would gorge themselves, sleep for six hours, then eat again before their kill rots and they must move on. Sen explained that most stories say that there are from twenty to thirty such abo bands roaming the back country of the four nations.

"I don't want to be the one to go in and take a census," Stone said.

They were still in a fringe of hills that worked toward the river, and now and then from a high point they could see the huge river ahead. It was so wide it looked like a big lake.

Once, they heard rifle fire from somewhere below. There were a few pistol shots, then silence.

Stone shrugged. There was no chance; they had to move forward. He took the point again and brought up Patterson right behind him. The tall G.I. from San Francisco was feeling better. He had eaten all the fruit. He was used to them from his years in the area.

"We gonna get a little action up ahead where those rifles were speaking, Sarge? Damn sure hope so. I got me a quota of ten slopes to waste for every year I was in their slammer. Think I'm gonna make it?"

"Hope we don't run into that many," Stone said. He grinned at the freedom smile Patterson wore and kept working ahead along the trace of a trail. They would know what the shooting was all about in the next half hour.

Chapter Nine

They stopped on a little rise from which they could see a ten-mile sweep of the mighty Mekong. Stone figured it was a mile wide right here. He knew that it began in Tibet and passed through China, Laos, and Cambodia before entering Vietnam and emptying into the South China Sea. The water highway was more than twenty-six hundred miles long. All Mark Stone and his party had to do was get across it.

Stone had decided there was no point in floating down the Mekong. It was a river to nowhere for them and was loaded with Viet and Cambodian river patrol boats. West, they had to move west.

As they took their break, Patterson questioned Stone. "Hey, who is president right now? Damn! I don't even know who my commander-in-chief is! Used to be Richard Nixon. Whatever happened to him, anyway?"

Stone told him.

"Christ! I bet my old man was pissed. He used to swear by Dick Nixon. Said he was the best president we ever had. Dad always liked the Republican presidents. He's loaded with money. At least he was when I left. Probably got more money now—yeah, it figures. You say the economy is going great? That means he's worth a few more million now than when I left."

Patterson slumped on the luxuriant growth of grass on the hill. "Damn! You know how great it feels to be free! Just to be able to sit here and not worry about the slopes, not worry about not getting fed, not to worry that them slant-eyed little bastards are going to pound you with another piece of bamboo? Did I tell you I have a lifelong mission to wipe out every bamboo plant in the world!" He laughed.

"You know how long it's been since I've really had a good laugh like that? Years and years and years. Hey, I got to figure out what in blazes I'm going to do after I get back to the States!"

Tears ran down his cheeks with the sudden realization. "I'm really going back. We're going to get there. I'm not sure I can take it. I've been locked up for so long!" He brushed at the wetness and swore softly.

"Hey, I'm scared. You know that? I'm fucking scared to death! I didn't even know who the president was. Who did you say, Ronald Reagan? Hey, didn't he used to be an actor, a movie and TV actor and now he's our president! You got to be kidding me!

"What I should do is get a stack of *Time* magazines and read each one, cover to cover. Thirteen years' worth—that would be more than six hundred. No chance. Girls. You still have girls out there? Pretty and soft and fun to kiss and snuggle up to? Thirteen years without a woman! My damn hand is near worn out!

"Damn! What about pay? I do get paid for all of those years, don't I? I went in as a staff; I should have had one, maybe two, promotions in thirteen years. What kind of money are we talking about here? I don't even know what the pay is."

Stone thought a minute. "A staff should get about $15,000 a year—that times all those years comes out to around $200,000."

"Don't shit me, man!" Patterson roared. "No lie? I'm gonna have $200,000 if I can walk into some U.S. military base somewhere?"

"That's about the size of it," Hog said. "Course as your agent I get ten percent . . ."

They all laughed and when they quieted they heard the angry stutter of an AK-47 somewhere not too far away. They all went on their faces into the grass and froze.

"Too damn close, Sarge. I better check it out." Hog lifted up.

Stone motioned him forward. "We'll both go. If they ain't looking for us, they sure as hell gonna be before long. We better cover our tails."

They moved like a pair of shadows down the trail toward the river. A single shot and a scream moved them off the trail toward a clump of trees to the left.

The two combat veterans bellied through the rotting vegetation to a point where they could see. It was a small clearing by a tiny stream. The first thing Stone saw was a cluster of children, all crying. A woman sat among them, trying to console them. Then, she was yanked from the group by a man holding a rifle and wearing green fatigue pants.

He stood her up and ripped open her blouse and a white chemise until her breasts swung out. The man grabbed one large breast, fondled it, and played with it. Then he laughed and pulled her toward the hut.

Stone saw two bodies in the clearing; one a large white man; the other a white woman who had been stripped. Her head lay at an odd angle as if her neck were broken.

Three more men came from a small hut set to one side. They all wore parts of military uniforms, but all different.

They were laughing. Stone nodded and both men lifted their CAR-15's.

"I've got the one with the woman," Stone said. He sighted in on the man's head and fired. The round caught him just as he turned to look at the woman. Instead of hitting the back of his head, the bullet slammed into his ear, drove upward through his brain and out the top of his head. The woman screamed and fell toward the children.

Hog's first round bored a small round hole through the heart of the man on the left who held a machete. He pivoted away and fell into the stream. The other two men lifted rifles, looking around for somebody to shoot. Two shots later those two fell to the jungle floor, dead and ready to decay.

The woman sat up. She looked like an American. She was taller than the Orientals, and now she talked to the children in English, trying to calm them. Her voice rose over their crying and questions, but it was soothing and caring.

"Lady, are there more of the murdering bandits in there?"

She turned, lifted her shoulders, stared in the direction of their voices.

"No, you have quite brutally murdered all four of them. They were Khmer Rouge deserters, peasants going back to work their farms."

Stone frowned. "They killed your friends over there on the ground and you're defending them?"

"Some things are hard to explain." She stood, told the children to stay where they were, and walked with a firm stride to the hut. She looked inside, then staggered and reached for the door, her face white with terror.

"Cover me, buddy!" Stone said. He ran for the hut, his finger on the trigger of the rifle, his eyes taking in everything around the clearing at once. He saw no more danger.

At the hut door he caught the woman just as she collapsed. Stone carried her to where the children were and laid her on the grass. Then he went back to look in the shack. The walls were spattered with blood. A woman lay naked on a thin pallet. Her hands were cut off, her breasts slashed, and a three-foot length of bamboo jammed into her abdomen.

Stone brought cold water from the stream and bathed the forehead of the unconscious woman. Slowly the brown-haired American with the torn blouse revived.

"Jennifer! Jennifer!" she shouted and tried to stand. Stone kept her sitting on the grass. She looked at him. "Jennifer, she's hurt badly. We must help her!"

"I'm sorry, miss, but no one can help her. The lady in the hut is beyond our help. She's dead."

"No!"

"Yes. The woman in the shack is beyond any kind of medical aid. Try to believe me."

Tears streamed down the lady's face. She made no effort to cover herself where her blouse had been ripped half off. One breast showed. She paled for a moment and a shudder went through her body. When she stared up at him, there was a different look to her eyes—colder, tougher.

"My name is Mary Eve Filmore and I'm from Philadelphia. I didn't catch your name."

For a moment they could have been in Philadelphia at a church social exchanging names.

"I'm Mark Stone, and we must get you and the children away from here before the shots bring Viet soldiers."

"Away? Soldiers?" She looked around her and for a moment, Stone was afraid she was going to go over the edge. She obviously was already in shock. She clung to her sanity and cried again. As she did, she leaned toward him and he caught her in his arms.

Hog watched for a minute, drumming his fingers on the stock of his CAR-15. His savage face scowled. "Sarge, we got to get the hell out of here. Gonna be gooks all over this place in a few minutes. Bet a buck we just picked ourselves up more damn baggage, the woman and the six kids?"

Stone nodded. He eased the woman away from him and wiped at her tears.

"Mary Eve, we need to leave right now. Are the children part of your group?"

"Yes! The children go with me! Don't you dare—" She stopped. "I'm sorry." She brushed the last of the tears away from her cheeks, looked down at her blouse, and turned as she covered herself. She tied one part of her blouse to another, holding it together.

"Now, the first thing we do is give Brother Charles and Sisters Jennifer and Beverly decent, Christian burials. Oh, dear, we don't have a shovel. We must bury them before we do another thing!"

Stone had a stab of pain. "You and they were missionaries in Cambodia. Were you prisoners?"

"No, not prisoners—missionaries of the United Christian Missionary Outreach Church. St. Louis is our headquarters."

"All of the Christian missionaries have been out of Cambodia for ten years."

"We were special. We were not political. They said we could stay and run the hospital. Brother Charles is my real brother. He is—was a medical doctor. A medical missionary, the most worthwhile work the good Lord ever gave anyone to do!"

"Yes, ma'am. About he children. They go with you. Some of them look like they are of mixed races."

"They all are, and they are my responsibility."

"Do any of them speak English?"

"Of course! They all do to a certain degree. Now, how do we go about burying these three sainted workers for the Lord?"

Stone stood, helped the woman up, and then in a sudden

move, ducked under her arm and slung her over his shoulder.

"The jungle takes care of burial detail, ma'am. Unless you want to join them underground. Kids—hey, you guys!" All six of the children turned to him.

"We're getting out of here. Follow me. You understand?"

"Of course, we do, Mr. Stone," the oldest, a girl about ten, said. The children stood quickly and formed a line with the youngest in front and the oldest in the rear. Hog fell in behind them and the strange little group hiked out quickly toward the main trail.

The woman was squirming and shouting.

"Put me down this instant! I will not leave my own flesh and blood in a filthy Cambodian jungle to rot and be eaten by animals! I simply will not!"

Stone ignored her and walked forward. When they came to the track they had been following, he set her down. He signaled for Hog to go get the rest of the party and spun the woman around.

"Mary Eve, do you want these six children to be slaughtered by the Vietnamese, or used for rifle practice as they try to run away through the forest or jungle?"

"Gracious no, of course not!"

"Then stop blubbering and yowling! This is a combat situation. We do not have time to stop and bury our dead. This is a war zone. At any time the Vietnamese could come rolling through here with ten to forty thousand troops. Am I getting through to your logic center, Miss Filmore?"

"You are, Mr. Stone. Remember that is my brother back there and two of my dearest friends. All I want to do is give them a decent, Christian burial."

"I know, Mary Eve. And if I let you do that, I'd probably have to give you and half my team a burial. I am not ready to throw away lives when I don't have to."

"You are a monster, a murderer! You didn't have to kill those men back there. You could have forced them to drop their arms and then run them off into the jungle."

"Miss Filmore, I am not a missionary or a social worker. I am a soldier by trade, and I know my business."

"Which is killing people."

"When I have to—especially to save the lives of other people like you."

"Oh. Yes, thank you for saving my life." Her voice was flat, cold, hard, impersonal.

"That is what I call sincere. Now, enough of the arguing. Where were you heading with the children?"

"To Thailand, to get them away from the fighting. We were moving our ministry into the refugee camps over beyond Aranyaprathet. That's in the near edge of Thailand."

"That is over two hundred miles away. What transportation do you have?"

"Our stamina and our strong legs and feet."

"It's a long walk."

The others came then, and quickly they moved down the trail, putting the woman and children in the middle of the line. They hiked toward the river, hoping they could get across while it was still daylight, and then hide on the far shore until darkness.

They made it along the rarely used trail to the river and began looking for some way to cross. Mary Eve said they had heard of a man with a boat along this stretch. That is why they came this way.

After a fruitless hour of searching for the man, they rested in some heavy brush near the road next to the river. The woman walked up to Stone and was angry again.

"Mr. Stone, I really am uncomfortable around all these weapons. These men are strange. Two of them say they were prisoners of war until last night. Is that true?"

"Yes. We came to rescue them and bring them home. Our helicopter was shot down."

"All of this is illegal, I presume, from what little I know of you."

"Entirely illegal, Miss Filmore. The U.S. government specifically forbid me from coming to the far east, and this country in particular. Does that bother you?"

"'Render unto Caesar,' Mr. Stone. 'Render unto Caesar.'" She frowned. Mark Stone felt strongly about the woman. She was honest, she was dedicated to her beliefs, and she was attractive in an interesting way. Her face was oval and her features almost severe, but when she smiled at the children, she had a glow, a beauty, about her that was hard to describe. She was tall and well proportioned and her short hair was a soft brown with glints of red in it.

"Am I disfigured, Mr. Stone? You are staring at me."

"Oh, sorry. I was wondering how long you've been in Cambodia?"

"Almost seven years now. When we came, no one thought we could get in. But faith can move mountains, so why couldn't it convince a few self-important Cambodians and Vietnamese that we could help them by educating some of their people? It worked. Our clearance papers came through. The four of us were going to remake Cambodia!"

"Why the change of mind?"

"The Cambodian government is a joke. The Vietnamese do anything they want to. They pressed all the fourteen-year-old boys from our village into their army. They took ten fifteen-year-old girls to be prostitutes for the soldiers. Then they came and burned down our church and children's home, just for the sport of it! Brother Charles prayed all night in the rain. In the morning he said the Lord told him it was time to move to Thailand and work with the half million Cambodians there in refugee camps. So we packed up."

"Packed?"

"We had a string of six water buffalo loaded down with our school equipment and the altar and Bibles. The first day out of Hoc Neu, bandits swept down and stole everything, including the buffalo. We decided to come on through anyway; we still had our lives."

"You have seven lives left, Mary Eve. Let's hope that you don't lose more of them before we get to Arany-aprathet."

Chapter Ten

Loughlin stepped in beside Stone who led the unit along the side of the road near the surging Mekong.

"Don't know what happened, Sarge. Hillburton just wigged out on me again. Had to take the rifle away from him and the knife. He thinks the Cambos are his Viet guards. Says he's going to kill them both and doesn't care what the other guards in the camp do to him."

"He's flashing back," Stone said, "reliving some of the bad times in prison camp. Not one hell of a lot we can do about it. Sit on him if you have to, but remember, he's the reason we came to this clambake."

"Right. I'll be as gentle as possible. How is it going with the Dragon Lady?"

"We're cold-blooded killers and sinners and that's just the start. We really got in trouble for not letting her bury her dead back there at the shack."

"We'd have all been dog meat by now if we had. I'll watch Hillburton closer."

Loughlin hiked back to his place in the line of march

and tried to talk to Hillburton.

"Doug, where you from?"

Hillburton looked at Loughlin and frowned, a serious expression showing. "Don't damn matter, got these two slopes behind me. They never gonna let me go. Be here forever. Rot right here, and nobody ever gonna know!"

"Doug, those two are Cambodians, anti-Communist guerrillas. They are part of our rescue team, remember? We broke you out of the prison camp. You're on your way right now to Thailand where we can get you a jet back home. You're a free man, Hillburton; try to remember the break-out."

"Damn, ain't you listening? Slopes won't let us go. Told you there are two of them right behind me. Little bastards hang in there. No way they gonna let any of us get out of here. I told you that before!"

"Easy, Doug, take it easy. Hey, say you could get back. What would you do? Stay in the service?"

"Hell, no! If I ever get back, I'll get me a little farm way up in the hills in Oregon. Sit up there and raise some trees. Yeah, Christmas trees. Have a few hogs, couple of steer for meat, and chickens. Always did like chickens. You like chickens?"

"Sure do, Doug, especially drumsticks."

"Well, I'd try to find a woman who would have me, I guess. Been so damn long, doubt if I would know what to do with one. Nobody would want to stay with me. Got myself all fucked up somehow. Damn slopes did it. Did something to my head. But the hogs won't care."

Loughlin looked skyward as Doug went on with his description of what he would do back home. Loughlin had a feeling the long story could last until dark.

Back at the front of the line, Sen tugged at Stone's sleeve and pointed to the river. A flat boat loaded with some kind of produce worked its way slowly down the river. It was on this side of the wide waterway where the currents moved more slowly.

"Try to get them to come ashore," Stone told Sen.

She ran at once toward the river and out on to the last bit of sandy soil she could find, waving a white piece of cloth she had evidently kept for just this purpose.

She called to the boatman. He swung his clumsy craft closer to the shore. Sen talked to him. Stone heard only a few of the words. The lone man on the boat at last shouted back, shook his head, and continued past them.

Sen dropped her hands in defeat and ran back to where the party had stopped.

"He say he has no motor. It would take him ten miles downstream to get us to the far side."

"And he was afraid?"

"Yes. Much afraid. Every stranger in Cambodia is a possible killer. To be afraid is wise."

They walked on, moving upstream away from what they thought might be a village to the south.

Mary Eve fell into step beside Stone. She wore slacks and hiking boots and matched him stride for stride.

"I am here to apologize, Mr. Stone. In my anger and showing no humility at all, I said bad things to you. I'm sorry. Sometimes I have trouble with a stubbornness and pride, two traits every Christian must battle most of her life."

"No apology is necessary, Miss Filmore. You only said what you believe and still believe. Our loyalties and our jobs here are slightly different. However, I see no reason we shouldn't help each other as much as we can."

She smiled. It was a charming smile. "Please," she said softly, "can't we get back to Mark and Mary Eve? I would like it so much better. I am not good for anyone when I am angry and upset about things."

"Mary Eve it is. How are the children holding up?"

Her smile came back. "The hope of Cambodia! If we can only implant in them the Christian teachings so they can help their country . . ."

She was beautiful, he realized. Part of the knot that held her blouse together had come untied. He looked away.

"I know, it's coming apart again. I . . . I want to thank you again. If you had not come when you did, they would have done to me what they did to . . . " She shuddered, then looked at him. "I was more terrified of being raped than of dying. I've never been so close to being forced that way. I actually fainted, didn't I? I've seen dead and dying before in attacks by guerrillas. I guess when it was . . . was someone I knew . . ." She turned away. "I am thankful that I still have my life. I thank you for that gift."

"I know it's been horrible for you," Stone said. "I think you're holding up remarkably well."

"It all is set out for us. I guess I have such a strong faith in God that I simply must believe whatever happens is by his design. It is simply God's will."

"Predestination? You're a fatalist? Then what does it matter what anyone does? We all should take the easy road. It doesn't make any difference what we do. What will happen will happen whether we bring it about ourselves or not. Why not give up?"

She chuckled. "You're a good soldier, Mark Stone, but not strong in philosophy or theology. It is still extremely important what a person does. We must strive and strive as much as we can. Only through that effort will God's will come out the way he wants it for us. Can you see the tremendous difference?"

"Some good can come out of your three friends being murdered?"

"'God moves in mysterious ways, His wonders to perform.'"

Stone laughed softly. "You're right. I'm not much on religious thinking, especially when it goes against my own logic and common sense. I'm sorry. Forget I said that. You know what impresses me most about you, Mary Eve? It's your eyes. I've never seen anyone else with eyes that reveal exactly what she is thinking. You must be careful with those eyes."

"Oh?" She watched him for a moment. "Right now these eyes are surprised and pleased and happy."

They walked along for several strides.

"Good, I hope we can be friends," Stone said. "From here to Thailand is one hell of a long walk."

"I want to be friends. But I wish you wouldn't put the length of our hike quite that way."

Stone laughed. "From here to Thailand is a tremendously long journey."

"Yes! Much better. Now, I must watch my small charges. They are very good at moving, and most have been under fire half of their lives, poor dears. I want to take them away from the danger, away from starvation." She smiled at him, touched his shoulder and went back to the children.

Sen spoke softly and pointed to the river.

"Down!" Stone whispered. The word passed back along the line. "Everyone get behind a tree or bush and stay completely hidden. A patrol boat is coming this way."

On the wide water a Viet patrol boat chugged with the current and headed toward their side of the shore. The boat, with machine guns mounted fore and aft, usually carried four Viet troopers. One steered and three worked the guns. They had a reputation for shooting up everything they saw.

The boat powered toward them and swung upstream slightly so it could turn close to the shoreline near where they huddled. The pilot of the small craft circled twice, and Stone could see one man using binoculars. At last, the boat turned and angled across the current to take them to the far side. When the boat was out of sight, Stone stood and waved his charges forward.

He put Sen on the point and moved back along the line,

checking on each person. Hog's shoulder was hurting him now, but he would not admit it. Stone could tell by the way he held his arm as he walked.

Patterson was holding up better than Stone expected. He gave him one more chocolate bar.

"Just in case you run out of fuel," Stone said.

"Hell, Sarge, I can run on empty for the next two hundred miles if I have to. Man, I can live on oxygen alone from here to Bangkok!"

Stone slapped him on the shoulder and checked the children. He absolutely would not get involved with them. He knew too well how the small ones could steal a man's heart. He saw that each one had strong shoes, and their clothes were neat and clean. That in itself was a small miracle.

He smiled at Mary Eve. "I need to talk to you on the way back. Can I have an appointment?"

She looked at an imaginary watch. "I'll be free about ten-fifteen." Then she smiled.

Loughlin was just behind Hillburton. The corporal stared at Stone but never saw him. He kept walking, stayed up with the march, but was in his own private fog somewhere.

Loughlin shrugged. "We get him home, we let some shrink work on him. Remember that P.O.W. who wigged out on us? By the time we got to Bangkok, he snapped out of it fine."

"Hope Hillburton can, too. How are the Cambodes?"

"Doing fine. They earn their pay. No complaints. Hell, I couldn't understand them if they did complain."

Stone walked toward the front, fell in step beside Mary Eve.

"You have a highly religious name."

"You noticed. My parents were missionaries. I was born in Africa in a state that isn't even there anymore. My father died there from some fever nobody ever diagnosed. He was a medical missionary, too."

"Runs in the family."

"If we find a boat, how do we handle the situation?" she asked after a moment's silence.

"We first try to rent it, to pay the owner to haul us across. If that doesn't work, we try to buy the boat. Next, we try to borrow it, and as a last resort we steal it or take it by force and give it back to the owner when we get to the other side."

"Because we're stronger than the owner is."

"We better be, or we'll all be dead. We can hide along this bank only so long; then the Viets, or the Cambodian units, or some more wandering bandits are going to surprise us. As you can see, we are not set up as an ideal fighting force. We have six professionals. We have one ex-P.O.W. who is gung ho and could get himself blown away. We have one ex-P.O.W. who is mentally unstable, and then we have seven civilians."

"I'm sorry we're a burden to you."

"Fortunes of war, Mary Eve. It can't be helped. We can't leave you and your six kids to play footsie with the murdering bas—" He looked up at her.

"Bastards, is the word you're working on. I've heard it before." She closed her eyes. "And I'm afraid you're right about leaving us alone. We couldn't last two days."

They walked several paces. He looked over and found her watching him.

"I've got to get back to the war; you take care." He walked back to the front.

"Where are all of the boats, Sen?"

She sighed. "Many move only on the river at night to avoid bad guys. They are smart guys."

"One is all we need, just one, even if it has to make two trips."

Stone saw a small rise ahead, less than two hundred yards from the water's edge. He angled his people up the slope and found that it was covered with thick growth that would hide them, yet there was a spot they could use as a lookout for a boat.

The men and kids settled down in the green growth and grass and rested. Stone put out two Cambodians as security. One went fifty yards upstream and the other one fifty yards below. Sen stood the first watch looking for a boat.

For a moment Stone leaned against a tree and closed his eyes. What he needed now was a small miracle. He snorted. Maybe he was in the right company to order his miracle. His options were limited. It would take them two days to build a raft with the one machete they had. Then they might float ten miles downstream before they could reach the other side.

Swimming was risky. Part of the Mekong was filled with hungry alligators. It had to be a boat. They had to wait.

As he watched the river, a five-man Viet patrol swung south along the cart road. They were not patroling, just marching fast in a rush to get somewhere.

That was one little bit of combat contact they had missed.

He saw two boats high on the river, but both of them were at the far side. Sen would not have a chance to talk to anyone aboard them. He tried to remember what it was that An Khom had said just as they left. Something about a contingency chopper, but there was simply no way to contact him to send one. That damn lucky bullet! It had saved his life, but that could be a temporary condition. He had fifteen passengers, including himself, and no damn bus to get them out of the country.

As he scanned the river, he saw a small boat hugging the shore on this side. It moved faster than the current, so it must have a motor. Sen saw it, too. She pointed at the river and he nodded. She vanished like a bird into the jungle and he saw her moments later hidden from the land mass behind a tree that grew in the backwater of the mighty Mekong.

The boat came along the same course. If it were a patrol boat, she would appear to be only another Cambodian fishing or hunting for some kind of roots that grew along the shoreline.

Stone stood and watched the boat coming. They would know very soon.

Chapter Eleven

The only thing that saved them was their position on the high ground.

Sen had just slipped back into the growth at the top of the hill after talking with the boatman. She motioned to Stone.

"Somebody saw me," she said. "Should have been more careful. Much sorry."

Stone gave a sign and everyone dropped to the grass and dirt.

Almost at the same time a volley of rifle fire erupted below and to the south as at least a dozen weapons spoke the language of death.

Stone looked over his charges. None had been hit so far. He motioned Hog to take the left flank. Loughlin already had moved to the right and Stone squirmed and crawled to a teak tree, then peered around it at ground level.

The firing came from the edge of a small bank below. It afforded cover for the attackers, and they were out of grenade range.

"Hold your fire!" Stone barked. These were regular Vietnam troops below them. Each man down there was concealed and protected by the bank. They would not show themselves unless they had to.

Outflank them, Stone decided. Maybe they did not yet have flankers covering them. How many in the attacking force? He guessed about sixteen to twenty.

He could protect the children if the band were no larger. But a concentrated attack by a company of Viets would be a disaster. Where did the bastards come from?

The rifles from below kept blasting, but with no pattern, not even a minor strategy.

"My turn," Sen said. She had crawled up near Stone. She had both of the Cambodians behind her. "We slip around side, blast them," she said.

Stone began to protest; then when he saw the look in her eye, he relented.

"Okay, just don't get hit. You're already wounded. We need you with us."

She smiled, gave him a thumbs-up sign, and worked rapidly down the back of the hill, away from the attackers.

"Let's keep them busy down there," Stone said. "Hog, Loughlin, blast them every ten or fifteen seconds. No pattern. Sen is making a flanking move for us."

The men nodded assent and went back into positions around trees where they were well protected.

Stone got Mary Eve's attention.

"Better take the kids down the reverse slope about fifty yards. We don't want a ricochet nipping any of the nippers. Keep your heads down and stay quiet."

Mary Eve began to say something, then stopped. She nodded and herded the children down the back side of the hill. Stone was surprised how quiet and orderly the children were.

He looked at the river. An empty flat boat with an idle

outboard motor on the rear floated down close to the near shore.

"Damn it!" Stone growled. There went a great chance to get across the river.

He pulled a grenade off his pack straps, jerked the pin free, and threw the small, smooth bomb as far as he could toward the patrol below. With the height of the hill, he got more distance than he hoped. The grenade came within ten yards of doing damage to the troops below.

Patterson cheered and tried one of his own. The big man threw the bomb like a baseball outfielder, exposing himself for three or four seconds. The grenade landed over a log some of the men had been using for cover.

"Bingo!" Patterson screeched. "Did you see that? I hurt the little sons of bitches! I must have wasted two or three of the damn bastards!"

Stone looked at the distance again. No wonder the Vietnamese were working slowly up the hill.

"They're away from the bank," Stone called. "Pin them down right where they are!"

The number of shots from the guns on the hill picked up, and the advance stopped.

Patterson threw two more grenades, and both times screams of pain followed the blasts. Stone was not sure if they were real or faked.

Sen had been happy when Stone said she could lead her two countrymen on an attack. They had run down the back of the hill in the heavy growth, then moved cautiously to their right toward the enemy.

She lay down in the oozing ground of the wet, marshy jungle floor and worked forward on her hands and knees. It was slow going with the big rifle over her back, but it was also safe. She had learned that a dead soldier does not do her unit or her commander any good at all. To fight, a soldier must be alive with a finger on a trigger.

She paused, parted some small bamboo shoots, and stared ahead. It was clear for another twenty yards. She led the two men forward to the next observation point she had selected, then wormed silently to the side of a betel palm, and looked around the shaggy trunk.

She could see the enemy!

The men hid behind logs and trees with a few still behind the cut of the small stream's bank.

That was when the first grenade went off. She figured Stone's people had thrown it. It was short. She waited. There would be more. When the next bomb exploded among the Vietnamese, she had worked out her attack plan.

Silently she motioned for one of the Cambodians to move to his right and find a firing position. She pointed to her spot for the other man and then worked her way with caution and patience to a place farther to the left.

She tugged a grenade from her pack strap. It was one that had the plastic explosive enhancement. Good! The grenade would be the signal to start firing. She held up the small bomb so the two Cambodians could see it; then she pulled the pin. She took a deep breath and with all her might threw the grenade with her elbow locked the way she had been trained.

The bomb sailed through the air, past a betel palm, and landed just in back of the log where three Vietnamese huddled. The blasting roar of the bomb sent birds skittering through the trees. It also blasted four of the enemy into hell and caused three of the survivors to turn toward them.

The Cambodian men brought up their CAR-15's and Sen lifted her AK-47 rifle, and they slammed two dozen rounds into the confused and outflanked Vietnamese. Three of them died before they could move. Four more rolled over the bank to the safety of the stream bed which was now barely a trickle of water.

Several more Viets began firing toward them. Sen felt

the whisper of a bullet pass her face. She ducked and looked from the other side of the tree. As she saw her attacker, he took a round through his forehead and folded.

Three men left their safety and surged forward, rifles on assault fire, forcing the three Cambodians to duck behind cover.

When the firing stopped, Sen looked out. She knew the Vietnamese had covered half the distance between them. Another charge and the Viets would be on top of them!

She pulled her last grenade and worked out the safety pin. She held it up so her men could see, then signaled that they would use only one small bomb.

Just then the men in green fatigues sprang up, rifles on full auto as they charged. Sen flipped the grenade forward as she lay flat behind a teak tree. The mere seconds to detonation seemed like a thousand years.

The four Vietnamese were in the final surge when the bomb went off. Two of them caught the most shrapnel and died at once. Another had his arm blown off and would die of lost blood in two or three minutes. The fourth took several deep slices from the shrapnel but remained on his feet. He charged the last five yards to his objective and surged around a tree.

As he did, Sen pushed up the already raised AK-47, jammed the muzzle into his chest and triggered off eight rounds. The soldier jolted back four feet as the bullets pounded into him. He was dead before he hit the ground.

Pressing hard against the side of the riverbank, Lieutenant Le Phat Vinh tried to recover from his surprise at the flanging attack. He had no thought of an aggressive move. He had lost eight to ten men in the sudden, deadly strike.

He shouted for his men to get back to the riverbank. They came rolling, crawling, falling over the ledge to the mud four feet below.

Vinh would not permit anyone to defeat him!

He would lose every man if he had to. The rebels, the deserters, whoever was hiding on the hill would be trampled down and squashed like bugs! He was an officer. He would *force* his men to be victorious!

He called his sergeant for a casualty report. A private crawled up and reported that both the sergeant and the corporal were dead. He had no idea how many men left could fight.

"Bastards!" Vinh shouted. He turned to the private. "You're the sergeant now; count the men, stupid!" Vinh would not permit his force to be defeated!

He ordered two men to work closer to the flanking force and throw four grenades into the area. They did it quickly, but Vinh could hear no cries of wounded. He scowled.

The hunter had become the prey. He would not retreat. He sent one man to circle the hill on the side away from the flankers and waited.

Two minutes later he heard a pair of rifle shots and a scream that could only be from his man.

Lieutenant Vinh counted his forces. He had begun with sixteen men. Now he had only six fighting troopers left. One man lay with a massive leg wound. He was worthless and was not counted.

Vinh thought of the promotion to captain when he would have a whole company under his command. This incident would not look good on his record. He would report that a major unit of the Khmer Rouge had hit him while he defended a vital road crossing. Yes, that would cover his losses!

But he would not pull out. He had to discover for sure who was on the hill above and what they were hiding from. They could be Rouge; they fought well enough. But the grenade had been a surprise. That one thrown by the flankers had been louder and more powerful than any hand bomb he had ever heard. Where would the Rouge get weapons and bombs like that? America? China? He had forgotten who supplied the hated Khmer with weapons this year.

Fire from above continued but at a lower rate. He had to do something. He still had six men, all had AK-47 rifles and plenty of ammunition. They had used up the last of their hand grenades. The men complained because they were too heavy to carry. Next time they would know better.

If there were to be a next time.

He would move his force to the left, the way his scout had gone. But they would be prudent and move without the loss of a man. One soldier would stay here with all of the rifles of the dead men. He would keep up a constant barrage of fire until his ammunition ran out. The hope was that the hiders on the hill would think the main force was still there.

It would be a classic ploy with deception as the main ingredient. And it would work! It had to work! Or all he had labored for, for so long, would be lost.

Vinh picked the strongest of his men, positioned him at the edge of the riverbank, and laid eight extra AK-47's along the bank on either side, each with a full, 30-round magazine. Vinh spoke quietly to the gunner and promised that he would be a corporal before the day was over. Then Vinh moved cautiously with his five men down the river to the heavy growth of bamboo that would shield his climb up the hill toward the renegades.

Sen had moved her two men as soon as they threw the grenades. The grenades of the enemy had not harmed any of her detail.

Now she had moved forward again until she could see the riverbank. To her surprise, only one man stood there. Another man lay in the mud, his leg bloody.

She watched a moment. The Viet picked up a rifle and began firing steadily at the top of the hill. When the rifle emptied, he moved to the next one.

Sen put a three-round burst of the 7.62mm rounds into the gunner. He spun away from the bank and fell face down in the stream. The Cambodian on her left fired at the wounded man, putting him out of his pain.

Sen signaled her team to pull back. They crawled away, then lifted up and ran through the jungle, went fast up the back of the hill, past where the woman and the children were, then slowly across the top of the hill so they would not be shot as enemy troops.

Stone saw her and waved; they moved in. She told him quickly that the men below had moved.

"They did not come our way. Must have moved downstream, over to the bamboo thicket."

Stone turned his binoculars on the thicket and smiled. He put the muzzle of the AK-47 toward the bamboo and fired a six-round burst. There was no reaction.

"Must be there, Sarge," Sen said. She found a position and motioned the two Cambodians to do likewise, and they settled down to wait for the Viets' next move.

Stone understood it. The force below had been cut in half by their attacks. Sen said their grenades had cut down six or seven. Now, the commander below was trying for a flank attack that would be a surprise, hoping he could overrun the hilltop.

Stone swung three of his men around so they could concentrate on the bamboo and where it thinned out to nothing. There would be twenty yards of naked ground to cover. He put his best grenaders on that end.

Now, it was up to the Vietnamese commander. Again, all Stone and his team could do was wait.

The wait was nearly a half hour for the hostages on the hill before the Viets made a move.

Stone had kept up a scattering of fire into the bamboo and across the face of the slope. He hoped to confuse the Viets.

Loughlin lifted his hand and pointed at the open place across from the bamboo thicket. One green-clad figure worked his way over the scalped area with infinite patience.

Stone gave Loughlin a thumbs-up sign and the big redhead put a three-round burst into the squirming figure. The man lifted up and tried to run for the bamboo, dragging one shot-up leg. Stone nailed him with six rounds and the small soldier's run for life was finished forever.

Now, Stone motioned for them all to fire into the bamboo. It did little good; the thick bamboo stalks soaked up the lead and protected the Viets. It did let them know that Stone knew where they were hiding.

The Viets sent an occasional volley at the hilltop, then quickly pulled down behind cover.

Stone realized they were in a stalemate, one that could easily end with fresh troops arriving for the Viets. No help was going to come for Stone's side. He had to move and move quickly. A plan began to form in his mind. It would take some luck, but they might just pull it—

Stone stared in amazement down the hill.

"What in the bloody hell?"

Loughlin waved frantically and pointed downhill.

Hog lowered his CAR-15 and began swearing.

Below them, halfway between their position and where Stone guessed the survivors of the Viet detail lay, marched Mary Eve Filmore with her six Cambodian children in close order behind her. The youngest came first with the oldest in the rear. Mary Eve carried a white flag and moved deliberately toward the Vietnamese position below, ignoring the occasional shot coming from the bamboo cover.

"Now would be a good time for one of your miracles, Mary Eve," Stone said, half expecting the Viets to begin slaughtering the innocents as they walked into their gun muzzles.

Chapter Twelve

Stone glowered in amazement at the tall woman as she strode directly at the terrorists and rapists who claimed to be an army. She would be cut down!

"Cease fire!" Stone shouted. The guns on the hill went silent as everyone watched.

Mary Eve turned toward Stone and smiled. "Thank you, Mr. Stone," she called in a surprisingly strong but calm voice. The lady had guts, Stone gave her that. She wasn't much of a soldier, but she had guts.

The guns on the other side had quieted as well. She walked deliberately to the bamboo in which the Viets were hiding and called out in Vietnamese. A short time later a voice answered. They were too far away for Stone to get the tone of the conversation. He heard only an occasional word, which made no sense to him.

Mary Eve turned toward Stone a few moments later. Her strong and clear voice came plainly across the eighty yards. "Good news, Mr. Stone! Lieutenant Vinh has agreed to give us free passage across the Mekong! He will give us a two-man escort all the way across Cambodia to the refugee camps in Thailand. Isn't that wonderful?"

She waited, straining to hear his response.

"Mr. Stone, do you hear me? I said we have safe passage, now. We don't need the guns anymore."

"I hear!" Stone shouted. "I don't believe. Have Lieutenant Vinh and his troops walk into the open and throw down their weapons. That will prove he is serious and can be trusted."

She turned and translated what Stone had said. There was a moment of talk; then Mary Eve hesitated. She looked up. "He says he can't do that, but we are promised on his word as an officer and a gentleman that we have safe passage. All of us, Mr. Stone. Please come out, Mr. Stone, so we can show him that we can be trusted."

Stone passed a hand signal. Loughlin lifted up and ran to the rear, twenty yards down the reverse slope, and went prone, his CAR-15 covering that area.

Hog followed him a moment later, taking with him the two former P.O.W.'s. Stone sent the Cambodians next, and he waited at the observation point.

"Mr. Stone!" Mary Eve called. Some of her self-confidence was missing in her voice. "They have given you a time limit. In one minute you must come out into the open."

"We can't do that, Miss Filmore," Stone shouted. He rolled to a new position but no shots came.

A man in green fatigues slipped directly in back of Mary Eve, using her body as protection. She looked over her shoulder. "Our time is almost up, Mr. Stone. Please cooperate and I'll get us out of Cambodia."

A sharp command came from the man behind Mary Eve, and twenty rifle shots sounded from the bamboo. Stone ducked behind his teak tree.

When he looked around it, Mary Eve was caught from behind by the green-clad figure. Rifle-toting guards rounded up the children and marched them into the bamboo cover. They knew Stone would not shoot if he might endanger the woman or the children. The man behind Mary Eve slowly tore the blouse and chemise from her shoulders, ripped it off her completely, and stomped it into the ground.

Her breasts swung free a moment as surprise and shock washed over her; then she covered them with her arms. The Viet soldier remained behind her, his protection from Stone, and using a sharp knife, cut off her pants and ripped them away. He took his time cutting off the cotton panties she wore. When she was naked, he spun her round and then spit over her shoulder in Stone's direction.

"Mr. Stone," the man who stripped her sneered in a surprisingly strong voice and in English, "we now have the woman, your woman I would guess. If you want her, come and get her!" Vinh laughed, caught Mary Eve by her breasts and pulled her with him into the jungle growth.

In impatient rage Stone pounded the ground with his fist twice, then turned and raced down the reverse slope, met his troops and sent them around the far side of the slope. He went the other way and soon spotted Vinh and his men leading their prisoners away. They marched north on the road.

The six Vietnamese were interspersed with the captives. There was no way to fire without hitting the friendlies and Vinh obviously was counting on that. Even the rear guard soldier was protected; he carried the youngest child in his arms.

Stone swore. He had arranged to meet his troops on the far side of the little hill. He did, and they marched north through the slopes of the small hills next to the Mekong. Vinh and his captives walked on the trail near the river. There was no chance to save them now. Perhaps when they camped for the night or arrived at some Vietnamese post . . .

It was soon evident the Viet lieutenant had a destination

in mind. They were still moving north. Stone called a halt.
He let everyone talk who wanted to about exactly what they
should do in this new situation.

Hog was positive about what they should do. "Hey, the
broad brought this on herself. We don't owe her anything.
Hell, the kids are natives; they'll survive; they'll get along.
Not even these bastards are going to shoot up a batch of
kids.

"I say we get back to our primary objective, rescuing
these two P.O.W.'s. And right now that means finding a
boat to cross the damn Mekong. Let the missionary get
herself out of the mess she got herself into."

Loughlin shook his head. "It is a pity, but we have a
duty to go after her. After all, we did rescue her once. We
indicated that we would help her get herself and her charges
out to friendly country. I don't see how we can turn our
backs on her now, even though she made a stupid move."

Patterson was still agog. "Man did you see them boobs!
That woman is stacked! Damn! Yeah. Well, I guess that we
should try to get her out. unless she winds up in the middle
of those forty thousand troops we've been hearing about!
That I don't want no part of. Hey, I'm gonna be rich if I
can just get out of this stinking hole! No suicide missions
for good old Sergeant Phil Patterson, no way!"

Hillburton did not respond when Stone asked him about
the woman. The Cambodians indicated through Sen they
had talked it over and that it was not their decision to make.

Stone stared at them all for a moment.

"We try to rescue her. It's a volunteer operation. You
Cambodians don't have to come. None of you have to. If
you want to help, fine. I can use you. Anybody who doesn't
want to help, just fall out and stay healthy until we're done.
For me, it's fish or cut bait right now."

Hog swore, pulled at his beard, and scratched his unruly
hair protruding from under the soft green cap.

"*Sheeeeeeet*. I guess we got to try to save the broad. Damn, I hate to waste good lead trying to save her pretty little ass." He snorted. "But she is an American. Hell, she's a P.O.W. right now, too, I damn well guess. We just have to get one more body out of the damn fire."

Stone punched him in the shoulder and then asked him how his arm was. He scowled and bit his lip. "Don't the fuck ask unless you want to know. And you don't want to know 'cause then I'd have to look at it to find out. It hurts. How the hell you think it would feel?"

"The pain has smoothed down your usual rough personality, at least," Loughlin said, a grin on his face. Hog swung at him and missed. Finally, they got back to marching their way north.

Stone sent one of the Cambodians out as lead scout. Sen told him to keep Lieutenant Vinh's party in sight. If they stopped or changed direction, he was to get back to them promptly. Sen, acting as a connecting file, worked ahead of the main party. She tried to keep both the scout and the group behind her in sight at all times.

They hiked north most of the morning and well into the afternoon. Sen sent up the other man to act as scout, and she said Vinh's party was pushing faster, carrying some of the smaller children. They must be trying to reach a destination before dark. It probably was an established camp.

Two hours before dark, Stone called in Sen. He had been laying out long-range plans. They included rescuing Mary Eve and the children, crossing the Mekong, and staying on a rough compass bearing for Aranyaprathet, Thailand. He looked at Sen.

"Would it be possible for one of you three Cambodians to get to the border alone? Could one of you get across the river and run to the border?"

She called up the other two Cambodians. The three talked about it after Sen translated. One man shook his head; the other bobbed his. Sen spoke sharply to them, then looked up.

"Vote is one yes, one no, one not certain. If Sarge wants somebody to go and contact An Khom, I am one."

Stone frowned. "We need you here."

"No need. Use signs to tell my countrymen what to do. Both smart. I can go. How far, only about two hundred miles? Not so damned long way. Might find water buffalo to ride!"

Stone scowled and rubbed his jaw. Loughlin said, "She's probably got the best chance. Knows the country, got the gumption."

"That's a long walk or a run," Stone said. "We need one of those iron men."

Sen was taking small items from the men and pushing them into her pockets.

"All decide. Sen go. Five days to the border."

"That's about forty-five miles a day!" Hog yelped.

"Easy. Sen marathoner—train long runs."

"I'll be damned," Hog said.

Sen smiled. "Anyway, other two no swim. Mekong come first."

Stone watched her. "Alligators," he said.

She shook her head. "Not here. Farther south, warmer water. They like small streams, too much current here. Gators lazy old bastards!"

"You can swim across the Mekong?" Stone asked.

"Yes. Float and swim. Tired, float. Then swim again. Not easy, but swim long way before."

Loughlin reached in his pack and took out a tough plastic airtight bag. He unfolded it, inflated it, and then he sealed it.

"Water wings," Hog said.

The air bag was two feet long and over a foot in diameter. It would easily hold up the tiny Cambodian woman. Her eyes glowed as she took it.

"Time to go now. Not dark."

She gave some things to her brother, then hiked down to the river, and stepped in. She had no weapon, no pack. She had tied the air bag tightly to one wrist by a short length of cord so she could not lose it and swam into the currents. She was pulled downstream at once but began moving toward the far shore. Before they moved on north, they saw her stop and rest on the air bag. She was relaxed and floating serenely downstream.

"Damn, I think she's going to make it," Hog said. "Know damn well I ain't gonna bet against her!"

They picked up their scout a quarter mile farther north. He was waiting for them. He indicated many smokes ahead, perhaps many Vietnamese camped.

They moved up slowly as Loughlin turned point man and then scout and hurried ahead to check it. He was back when they were a mile from the smokes.

"Whole piss-pot full of gooks up there. Must be some kind of an area base. I'd say Lieutenant Vinh would be sending back here for fresh troops. Suggest we outmaneuver the bastards right quick."

Stone struck due east into the jungle, then worked north again, and came out on a small hill that overlooked the Vietnamese camp a half mile away.

Loughlin had been checking it with the binoculars. He yelped and looked harder.

"Christ! London Bridge is falling down! Nine, ten, eleven—and even dozen. Guess what we have out there in that camp, mates?"

"Dancing girls?" Patterson asked.

"An elephant parade," Hog guessed.

"Almost, pal. There is a batch of twelve Soviet T-54 tanks. As soon as more roads around here dry out, those babies are going to be pure hell."

Stone checked through the long lenses. "Trouble—you're right. We better go up for a closer look." He checked his fighting troops. Two Cambodians, two pros, two ex-P.O.W.'s, and himself. Seven of them against a camp that could hold at least four thousand. He shrugged. The odds sounded about right.

"Let's all go for a close look and establish a base of operations. If they're looking for us, it would be to the south along the river. They know how that we need to cross over, thanks to our Miss Missionary. How in the world she could ever honestly think she could negotiate with a batch of rabble like these Viets I'll never understand! It had to be her religious training, I guess."

Loughlin agreed. "What's also bugging me is the size of the patrol? The Viets are damn stingy. Two or three to a company, not seven or eight like an English company of infantry would have. It looks like that patrol was looking for something special, maybe us. They seemed to know where to look."

"You Brits always have been rank happy," Hog said lifting both his hands to ward off a Loughlin blow. None came and Hog winced when he let his wounded arm down.

He glanced at Stone. "Don't ask!"

They worked to within a hundred yards of the clearing hacked out of the edge of the jungle. The camp was squatting on what had once been fertile rice paddies, all diked and terraced. Now, the land was hard and dry and would stay that way as long as the camp remained there. It meant the troops had to cut back only a hundred yards of former jungle to lay out the camp. There was rows of big twenty-man tents. Maybe two hundred of them laid out in company streets. He saw a few jeeps and the lumbering, ominous tanks. Oddly enough, he didn't see a lot of troops moving around.

The fuel dump had hundreds of barrels, probably filled

with gasoline and diesel but, stacked at the jungle side of the camp. They obviously had been brought in by ship, then loaded on flatboats, and rolled to their current position. Stone noted where the tanks were parked and the fuel stored. Both should come in handy later, either on the way in or out. At least, he hoped he could use them. The tanks were enticing.

Stone settled down to mapping the place. Loughlin had the glasses, watching for any sign of Mary Eve or the children. With any luck they would find their target location before they charged into the camp. Stone wanted to go in as soon as it grew dark. That would give them a small advantage. He could see some light towers but they would be negated.

There was no fence and no mine field—at least not one that was marked. Stone knew it would be simple to get into the camp. But finding Mary Eve and getting out with her and the kids would be the major problem.

They talked about the kids.

Hog pounded one big fist into his open palm. "Sen told me the kids would be sent right through the camp to the nearest village. The small ones would be dumped on the village chief. He'll have to find families to take them in. They'd want them to grow up a few more years. Then, the boys would be conscripted and the girls put into prostitute houses for the army. Some of these Viet commanders get all soft and sentimental about small children, Sen said."

"She was sure of all this?" Loughlin asked.

"True," Hog went on, "she says we can forget about rescuing the kids. They are long gone and we'll never see them again. Neither will Mary Eve."

Loughlin grunted, then handed the glasses to Stone.

"I think we just got lucky," the big Englishman said.

Chapter Thirteen

Grinning, Loughlin handed the binoculars to Stone. When he focused the lenses, Stone saw Mary Eve dressed in a dark green Viet camouflage uniform with sleeves and legs rolled up. She stood outside one of the tents that had four guards around it. A man with bars on his shoulders seemed to be telling her something in a friendly fashion.

She looked stern, lifted her brows, and walked into the tent. One of the guards closed a wooden door built into the front of the tent and snapped shut a padlock.

Stone used the glasses to track back to the nearest camp boundary. Her prison tent was on this side of the area, about a third of the way into the camp and fifty yards past the tanks. He set the place in his mind so he could find it in the dark.

"Loughlin, you spotted the generator tent yet? They must have juice at a place like this."

"Got it, leader. It's too far inside the camp for me to get in and out unseen after planting the radio-detonated charges. Thought of using one of the Cambodes, but guess I better get as close as possible and rely on the special plastic explosive grenades. One of them will do it, if I've got arm enough."

"You'll manage. We work better in the dark. Already I can spot the floodlights they have set up. Seen anything of the kids?"

"No chance the small ones are still in the camp. Probably shipped them out the way Sen told us. Probably sent them to a village where they have firm control. The kids'll get pushed around a little, but they're young enough; they'll adapt. I'll bet a penny to a pound the small ones have been sent down the road already and some old mama-san has them under her wing."

"Then, we don't look for them," Stone said. "We'll have enough trouble getting Mary Eve out of there." He studied the approach. There was no barbed wire, no fence around the camp. There were orderly rows of tents, big ones that reminded him of the U.S. Army's twenty-man field tent. There were dozens of fires, which seemed to be contained in some type of stove inside some of the tents.

No thatched roofs here to burn and light the scene. So he would keep it all dark. Yeah, dark and dangerous. That way he could take the two Cambodes along, keep them close by for support. Patterson could stay at the base of operations and give them support fire. If they could spot the camp headquarters or the commander, Patterson could bombard that tent with riflefire to add to the confusion.

Worth a try. As the plan unfolded he talked to Loughlin, Hog, and Patterson.

"Christ, let me get in there and kill more gooks!" Patterson yelled. "You guys owe me. I've been waiting for this for thirteen damn years! No way you can cut me out now!"

"You'll be sick of killing these slants by the time we're finished," Hog told him. "Just hold tight until we get the details worked out." Hog was scowling and Patterson backed off a step and listened.

"My primary target is the generator tent," Loughlin said. "When I have that blown and the lights go off, I'll stash a few extra grenades and thermites around to spice up the affair, then try for a meet."

"Right," Stone said. "Get your ass to Mary Eve's tent and help us pull a retrograde into the greenery. Can you handle that all alone?"

Patterson swore. "All I get to do is wham away into some tents? I won't know if I hit anybody or not."

"That's what will make it all the more effective," Stone said. "They won't know where all the fire is coming from. Get Hillburton to fire, too, if you can. You think he'll shape up to help? Was he ever this way in camp?"

"Doubt if he'll come around. He got this way sometimes in the compound. Once or twice a good slap on the chops would bring him out of it."

Stone weighed the chances. "Try it, Patterson, just before you start your mission. Tell him you need him. Might work. Have an AK-47 all set up for him."

It took Stone a half hour to get across to the Cambodian guerrillas what he wanted them to do. At last, they understood. One would stay within arm's reach of Stone, the other near Hog. They would fire to defend both men and at any target that presented itself. They understood it was a mission to rescue the missionary woman.

The sun died in the green jungle's hungry maw.

Loughlin took his CAR-15 and a shoulder pack with twelve souped-up grenades, four CAR-15 magazines, and he headed through the jungle along the edge of the camp to the spot where he could get closest to the generator. He had made the trip once in the daylight, staying in the cover. Now, it would be easier.

The first grenade blast would be the signal for the rest of the attack to start. Hog and Stone each had six grenades and four extra magazines. The Cambodians had two grenades each and four magazines.

Stone checked his watch. Loughlin had been gone for only five minutes.

Stone found Hillburton and told him what they were doing. The man shrugged and looked away. Stone slapped him twice, once forward and again backhand. It was not gentle treatment and Stone's hand stung.

"Hillburton, damn you! We need you to help us. You might not get home if you don't help us right now!"

Hillburton's memory of the authoritative voice and the anger roused something in the ex-P.O.W. He shook his head, touched his face, then blinked, and looked around.

"What the hell is going on?" he asked softly.

"Welcome back, Hillburton," Stone said. "We busted you out of prison, remember? You're a free man. Now, we got a little war game to play. Patterson will explain the whole thing to you."

Patterson punched the other ex-P.O.W. on the shoulder and began laying out the situation.

The four on the attack squad moved down to the very edge of the camp, where the jungle had been hacked to pieces, and waited. They crouched low, not more than fifty feet from the nearest tent. No one seemed to be in this one.

Lieutenant Vinh brought Mary Eve's food himself. It was from the officers' mess and the best rice and chicken they had in camp. Also, he carried a small bottle of rice wine and some fruit. It should please her. Vinh thought of his slender, delicate wife and smiled. She was nothing like this American with the big tits! He had never seen such breasts! Never had he seen such long, beautiful, marvelous legs!

The food would make her happy.

The guards had the door unlocked by the time he left the Jeep, and he stepped through the tent's door slowly, watching for some kind of displeasure. The tent had two electric lights, a pallet to one side, and two small wooden stools.

Mary Eve sat on one of the stools. She looked at him with disdain.

"Get out!" she shouted. "And take that food with you. I won't eat anything you bring."

Vinh made sure the door was closed behind him; then he dumped the food on the ground and strode to her. He grabbed her long brown hair and pulled her to her feet. In the same motion he spun her around and held her body against him with one arm, and his right hand closed around her breast.

"If you won't eat food, then you'll have to eat me, strange American woman!" He pulled at the shirt, popping off the buttons and tearing it away from her shoulders. Soon she was topless.

She had raked her fingernails down his cheek, leaving two long, bloody scratches.

"You filth!" Mary Eve screamed. "I'll never let you touch me."

She darted away from him. Vinh marveled at the way her big breasts jolted and bounced from the movement. He cut her off in the sparsley furnished tent, grabbed her around the shoulders, and forced her to the ground.

Short stubble of the last rice grown there stabbed into her knees and then her back. The jolt of hitting the ground left her a little dazed. Then she blinked and knew she was on her back. The man was pawing at her crotch and his mouth was on her breast, sucking and chewing.

She tried to heave him off.

Vinh only laughed. He got her pants unbuttoned and thrust his hand inside on her bare thigh and then drew it up to her crotch.

'No!" she shouted. "No!"

His hand dug deeper.

She watched his head. When he turned it, she pulled up

her head and grabbed his ear in her mouth, her teeth claming on it firmly. He screeched but didn't move his hand.

Mary Eve bit down hard, felt blood ooze into her mouth. Then spit out a piece of the top of Vinh's ear. This time it was Vinh who screamed. He sat back on the ground and stared at her. Then, from his pocket he pulled a small, folding knife with a sharp blade. He moved toward her.

"Now, American with big tits, we'll see how brave you are!"

The cracking roar of the first grenade came, then another and another. Stone and his men moved out, running hard to the first tent. The lights around the outside of the camp flickered, then went out. Slowly the rest of the floodlights dimmed and failed.

There were yells, orders snapped out, and they heard men running hard, shouting to each other.

The four moved slowly through the alley formed between ropes as if they belonged there. They passed the tanks and found only one shadowy Viet guarding them. The tanks were in various stages of readiness. In the bright moonlight, Stone could see one with its tracks off. Another had the cannon removed.

They rushed down the street now, met three Viets who shouted a question. Stone caught it, yelled over his shoulder in his best Vietnamese that he didn't know, and they kept going.

Two more of the tent streets to pass before they came to the right tent. Stone found it and saw two guards on the door. He walked up to one. Hog took the other. Without warning two knives flashed, and the Charlies blood soaked into the ground as the guards died beside their posts.

Hog sliced the side of the tent with his bloody fighting knife and peered inside.

"Mary Eve," he called.

A pistol fired from inside the tent, the round cutting a neat hole a foot from the slice. Hog went through in a dive. The inside of the tent was faintly lighted by a dropped flashlight. It sent a slender beam against the far wall. The gunman had shot at the sound of Hog's voice.

He lay on the ground holding his breath, listening for the enemy.

"He's to the right of the cut in the tent," Mary Eve said, her voice strangely calm.

Vinh growled and fired a shot at Mary Eve's voice. Hog was up and charging, his foot kicked out where the muzzle flash still burned a brightness in the dark.

His boot caught Vinh's upper right arm and spun the weapon out of his hand. Hog grabbed at the little man who scuttled away.

"Mary Eve, get the light. Shine it on him!"

Already she was moving toward the flashlight. Now, she grabbed it and swung it around the tent until she pinned Vinh at the far side, his knife jammed through the heavy canvas, making an escape slice.

Hog roared and charged him. He used hs momentum and his weight and slammed out a hammerlike fist, striking with the bottom of the fist into the screeching Vietnamese's chest. It bowled the officer over on his back, but he rolled and came up still in the light beam.

Hog jolted him with a kick that snapped Vinh's body sideways with the force. Hog followed it with a leap which caught Vinh on the side of the jaw and slammed him backward to the ground.

The big man roared as he jolted forward, leaping last three feet, his right arm raised. He smashed downward with his elbow, slamming down with fury and 210 pounds of weight, crashing into Vinh's chest.

Two ribs cracked. Two more broke and then snapped and were driven downward by the elbow's tremendous force until they pierced the Vietnamese lieutenant's heart.

Vinh died after two gasps, his eyes bright with surprise.

"Mary Eve," Hog called, "are you all right?"

"Yes, almost. Help me back into my shirt."

She gave him the light. He shone it on her before he realized she held the shirt in her hands. She did not move to cover her breasts.

'Oh, sorry." He shined the beam away.

"Mr. Wiley, my shirt is all tangled up. Move the light back so we can straighten it. I'm sure you've seen a woman's breasts before."

"Yes, ma'am." He brought the light back; they pulled the shirt right and she slipped it on.

"The electric lights went off. Are you attacking?"

"We came to get you, Miss Filmore."

"Good, oh, good. Now, where are the children?"

"We better get outside. Stone will tell you about that." He took her to the slit in the side of the big tent he had come through and held it as she stepped outside.

Stone took her hand as she came through the opening. "Mary Eve, we have to be quiet," Stone said. "It could be a long walk out of here. I don't want any argument and no noise."

"Where are my children?" she asked, her voice high, hysterical.

"They marched them north out of camp. They'll take them to a village where they will work back into the Cambodian culture. They are gone. We have no way to find out where they are and no time to go get them."

"No!" she screamed. Stone put his hand over her mouth. Her eyes flared at him in the moonlight.

"Quiet! You want to get us all killed?" Slowly he took his hand off her mouth.

"I can't leave without my six children! I simply won't leave! Do you know what they will do to those children in a Cambodian Communist village? They will be lucky if half of them live a year."

"Mary Eve, look at me. The children will have a ten times better chance of living where they are now than if we tried to get them. We all may die before this is over. If the children are with us, they are the enemy, too, and they will die. Now, they have passed over; they have been turned back into civilians. They are safe."

Mary Eve refused to accept the statement. "I won't go without my babies! I helped at the birth of nearly everyone of them! Their mothers entrusted them to me to get them out of Cambodia. I simply won't go. You can't force me. I'll scream all the time!"

Hog had stood there listening to the argument. He moved up behind Mary Eve and hit her in the side of the neck. He knew exactly how to do it so there would be little danger and maximum effect. Mary Eve fell unconscious into Mark Stone's arms. He lifted her over his shoulder.

"Let's haul ass," he said. The Cambodians understood that term. They had just turned to retrace their steps when a Jeep with its lights on raced toward the tent.

They eased back into the darkness. When three men in the Jeep ran for the tent with the ripped side, Hog hosed them down with a figure-eight pattern from his CAR-15. Two died in the hail; the third lifted a .45 and got off one round before Hog blasted six more .223 caliber rounds into the colonel with the eagles on his shoulder. Hog and the others ran for the Jeep; the Cambodians jumped in.

Hog checked the rig. No keys were needed. He hit the starter and Stone sat in the front holding Mary Eve. He had pulled the eight-shot SPAS shotgun off his back. It had the primary safety off and was at the ready.

Hog turned out the Jeep's lights and worked his way down the company streets. They had heard it before, but now the firing from outside the camp came more clearly.

Two AK-47's were chattering, pumping rounds into various parts of the base, but staying away from the section where Mary Eve had been held.

They turned down the street where the T-54 tanks were parked. Hog lifted his brows. Stone looked at the clanking death machines.

"Give them a look," Stone said. Hog parked the Jeep and ran for the closest tank that looked intact. Two men stepped out to challenge him but one round from Stone's SPAS shotgun turned both their chests into mashed hamburger and dumped them backward.

As soon as the rumble of the scatter-gun faded, Stone heard the new element: shuffling, men moving with weapons. The Cambodians lay down beside the Jeep. Stone pushed the unconscious Mary Eve down on the Jeep's front seat and went belly down to the ground beside the small natives.

They waited until the squad of fifteen Viets had moved cautiously to within thirty feet of the Jeep. Then, Stone fired two rounds from the scatter-gun. The Cambodians snarled several rounds into the shattered, struggling mass of terrified troops. Only two survived to race to the rear and raise the alarm.

Hog poked his head out of the top of the tank.

"Damn thing works. Operational! If I can get the bastard diesel engine started, we'll roll! Climb on. Take me about ten seconds." He vanished and a few moments later the starter meshed and the glow plug glowed and suddenly the shooting and grenading found a new sound: the clattering, roaring voice of a diesel tank engine as it warmed up.

They ran for the top turret and slid down. Then they lowered Mary Eve down and inside. Stone found the gunner's position, opened the slot, and peered through. He checked the big cannon, figured out how to fire it, and slammed a round into the breach. The gun swung around. He aimed at the tank farthest away from him, checked his procedures, and fired. The metal monster they now rode kicked back three feet, and the tank across the square exploded in a roaring, belching inferno as the ammunition inside it detonated in a series of continuing blasts.

The tank began to move.

Stone turned his attention to the machine guns. He tested them by firing through a tent. Then he moved them around and sprayed a dozen more tents. Down the way he saw forty Vietnam regulars moving toward the tank. The machine gun pounded big rounds into them. They felt like fifties going off, but Stone wasn't sure how big they were. The heavy slugs reduced the forty fighting men to ten who scurried out of the way.

They could her explosions outside through he clanking and roaring of the tank. Loughlin must be unloading the rest of his grenades, Stone figureed.

Stone had one of the Cambodians throw another big round into the cannon and he looked for a target. He settled for a row of tents and fired. The round tore through three before it hit anything heavy enough to set off the fuse train. The explosion came as a cracking roar that showered shrapnel over half the camp.

A Jeep raced across an alley between tents, but Stone had no chance to fire at it.

"Get up to that street and turn that way," Stone shouted to Hog who was having more fun than he ever had smashing into cars in a demolition derby.

He took a short cut, mashing through three of the twenty-men army tents and coming out on a road. Stone had another cannon round loaded now, and down the street he saw the brake lights as the Jeep slowed. He estimated the range and pushed the firing button. The round caught the Jeep on its bumper, which detonated the round, blasting the Jeep into spare parts and showering burning gasoline over a dozen tents and setting them on fire.

Stone felt something hit the tank and then knew it was a man who was scrambling up on it. He checked to be sure the top was closed and locked. Then he looked out the firing slits and saw the comic upside-down face that belonged to the intrepid Britisher, Terrance Loughlin.

"Going for a bloody ride without me?" he asked. "Did you get the bird?"

"Yes, Mary Eve is inside." Stone shouted at him so he could hear. "You want in?"

"Damn right, we're taking rifle fire."

They popped the turret top and Loughlin slid down and checked on Mary Eve who was still groggy.

"Place is jumping out there. Not nearly as many men here as we thought. Looks like some kind of a staging area. It's mostly empty yet."

A dozen rounds glanced off the tank, doing no real damage.

"I hope they don't have any RPG's or those shoulder-fired rockets," Loughlin said.

Stone chattered off a half dozen bursts with the machine guns. Then Hog spun the tank around in a circle. Stone sent six-round burps into the tents and any target he could find.

They all heard the new sounds almost at the same time.

"Mortar," Stone said. "No warning. That's not us. It has to be the Khmer Rouge. They're the only ones with that kind of firepower around here beside the Viets."

The explosions were heavy, loud, and deadly.

"Our diversion," Loughlin crowed. "Let's get his shuttle bus out of here and pick up our two paying customers just over the line into the greenery."

Stone tapped Hog on the shoulder. "Take us back home, James. We'll pick up our two ex-P.O.W.'s and head for the river."

They had moved forward, mashing down six more of the big tents, when Stone sucked in his breath. Directly ahead of him was a pair of Vietnam regulars belching death from a flame thrower.

Chapter Fourteen

Stone looked through one of the ports just as the flame thrower shot a deadly stream of burning liquid toward the tank. It fell ten yards short.

He swung the machine gun up and pulled the trigger.

Nothing happened.

"Jammed?" asked Loughlin who was crowded in near Stone.

"No, dry!"

Hog ran the tank motor and it charged ahead, picked up speed, and aimed directly at the flame thrower.

"Button up!" Hog yelled. "We gonna wipe out that son of a bitch just like in a destruct derby!"

The tank churned forward. Stone closed the gunner's slots and a moment later they could feel the heat as a flood of flaming gasoline washed over the outside of the tank. The shot failed to enter any of the ports or hit any of the vital parts of the monster.

Then, through the grinding and clanking of the tank, they heard a scream and felt a slight jolt as one of the treads ran over the man with the flame thrower and his big back tanks. Then the scream was dead and they lumbered toward the edge of camp.

"The fuel dump!" Stone shouted.

Hog nodded and swung to his left. He charged across six more tents until he found a spot from which they could see the fuel dump.

More of the heavy mortar rounds came in at the far side of the camp. There seemed to be infantry fighting involved on that perimeter as well.

Stone swung the big cannon around and sighted in on the large stack of barrels four hundred yards away. He adjusted the range, then fired.

The tank jolted backward a foot, then settled. Through the machine gunner's slots they saw the round strike and penetrate a dozen barrels, then detonate. A microsecond later, the explosion of the shell was followed by the *whoosh*-ing roar of a million gallons of fuel, as it all erupted in the largest single blast most had ever seen.

Hog turned the tank and rumbled away from the spot. He charged across a neat line of tents, snarling ropes and dragging down a dozen tents. Soon the tank trailed a dozen ropes around the tank and the tracks.

If they had been cables, they would have derailed the driving tracks, but the soft ropes were simply chewed up in the gears and tracks and the tank rumbled forward.

Hog approached the outer boundary of the camp and stopped.

"Visitors," the big man with the wild hair said.

Stone looked out and saw the forward elements of an infantry attack. Thirty men were spread out in an assault formation. They stood, ran forward to the edge of the camp, and dropped down.

Then, riflefire began hitting the tank.

"They think we're with the Viets!" Hog shouted. "Who are they?"

"Must be some more of the Khmer Rouge," Stone said. Turn this thing around and we'll fire some cannon shots into the Viets. That might convince the troops not to grenade us as we go by."

Loughlin loaded, Hog turned the tank around by freezing one track, and in a few seconds they were facing into the camp. Stone picked the first gathering of troops he could find and fired. Then, they fired four more rounds through the tents at close range. When Stone told Hog to turn the rig around again, he had the muzzle of the big gun as high as it would go. There was no chance that the tank could fire at the troops just in front of them.

"Damn!" Stone shouted. "What about Patterson and Hillburton?"

The Khmer Rouge troops swept by the tank without firing another shot and ran into the camp, probably surprised that there was no opposition.

Hog turned south and moved a hundred yards before he found the assembly point where they had left the two ex-P.O.W.'s. He jolted the tank in slowly, saw that they were past the forward lines of the Khmer Rouge troops, and ground up to the assembly position.

Nothing. Stone rotated the gun so he could see more, but found nobody.

"What happened to them when the Khmers came boiling through here?" Stone asked.

"I'm going out to find them," Loughlin said. He popped the top and crawled out. Stone was right behind him. They dropped to the ground and found the exact place they had been before.

There was no sign of the two men.

'At least we haven't found their bodies," Loughlin said.

"You go left; I'll go right," Stone said. "Check it out." They split and began combing the jungle, moving plants and vines and small trees. Stone found a Russian canteen, the same kind they had brought along.

He moved ahead.

Twenty yards farther along he heard voices. Stone crept silently through the murky, soggy jungle. He pushed aside some ever-present bamboo and saw two Orientals working over a small hand radio. They changed batteries, grunted, then made several transmissions, and received replies. They had to be Khmers. A moment later they picked up their packs and guns and hurried toward the north, skirting the Viet base.

Still no Patterson.

Then a voice cut through the black silence.

"Where did the Los Angeles Dodgers once play baseball?" The voice came from high overhead somewhere.

"Patterson, that you? They were from Brooklyn. Hey, are you in one chunk?"

"Yep—if we can get down from this damned tree without breaking a leg."

Stone followed the sound of the voice and spotted Patterson dropping from a small teak tree that had limbs close enough to the ground for climbing. Hillburton was just below him. When they got to the ground, Patterson grabbed Hillburton by the arm and led him to Stone.

"Safe and sound, Sarge!"

"What happened?"

"We saw the fuckers sneaking up when we was firing. We cut it off and moved back; then they kept coming so we went up the damn tree and they never once looked up. Guess they was going to attack the base out there, too. Who the hell are they?"

"Probably Khmer Rouge. They used to run the country. Then they got beaten out and now are trying to get it back. How is Hillburton?"

"About three magazines after he started firing, he looked over at me, said 'what the hell,' laid down, and curled up. I been pushing him around since."

"Damn, I hoped he snapped out of it. Hey, you guys want a ride? We appropriated one of those T-54 tanks."

Twenty minutes later they all met back at the tank. The war was getting hotter around the far side of the camp. The Khmers had swept across the near edge, which evidently was filled with nothing but empty tents. Now, the down and dirty infantry fighting was concentrated to the north. The heavy mortars had stopped falling, and the foot sloggers had taken over.

"Let's get out of here and move south," Stone said. When they tried to get in the tank, everybody wouldn't fit. Stone checked on Mary Eve. She was conscious and so upset that she would not even speak to him. She huddled near the empty ammo locker and folded her arms across her shirt and glared at him.

Stone and Loughlin rode on the outside of the tank, guiding Hog where he couldn't see. Soon they were below the camp and on the trail used by carts. It was a highway compared to sloshing through the jungle.

"Wish this thing would float," Hog groused from the driver's station. "Hell, then we could blast right across the damn river and charge on for Cambodia."

"After we pulled in at a petrol station," Loughlin said. "Any idea how much fuel we have?"

Hog studied the gauges, then swore. "About a dozen dials and readouts, but I don't know what the Russian words mean. At least, none of them reads empty."

Stone had determined that the farther south and away from the base camp the better. The Viets would have Jeeps out in the morning hunting for them . . . if the Viets won the battle now in progress. There was nothing else Stone and company could do until daylight. Even if they could spot a boat on the river, the boatman would not come to shore to talk to strangers, especially foreigners.

Loughlin spotted the hill where they had been ambushed,

and a mile farther down the shore of the big river, the tank
wheezed, grumbled, and clanked to a halt.

"Out of juice," Hog said. "All ashore who are going
ashore."

They unloaded from the tank.

Stone and Loughlin were the last out. They had grouped
a small stack of the cannon shells, three hand grenades with
C-4 and stacks of small arms ammo onboard. Loughlin had
rigged the last grenade to be lowered by a string from the
turret.

"Sure this will work?" Stone asked.

"Hell, yes, done it a hundred times," Loughlin said. He
snorted and grinned. "Well, I tried it once in France."

Loughlin leaned over the top of the tank from the outside.
They had moved everyone back a hundred yards. Stone was
half that far, watching Loughlin. He lowered the last grenade. The string was all that held the arming handle in
place. He put the trigger bomb on top of the other two, then
let up the pressure on the string.

Loughlin leaped off the tank. His feet were running before he hit the dirt. He took three long strides and dived
away from the tank.

The first grenade set off the others and the C-4 lacing,
which was enough to cause a sympathetic explosion of the
cannon shells.

Flame and smoke gushed from the tank, and one shell
burst halfway through it before exploding.

Loughlin hit the dirt and began crawling as fast as he
could, still keeping low to the ground.

Thirty seconds later it was over. The Russian T-54 would
be of no use to either side in the bloody little war.

Stone helped Mary Eve stand from where she had sat
down to wait for the others. She stumbled and he caught
her. She clung to him, her tear-stained face turned up to
him, and in the moonlight he saw that her mood had changed.

"They took my babies away," she said softly. "Whatever am I going to tell their mothers?"

Stone led her to the front of the small line of march that had formed and they walked south.

He put his arm around her shoulders. She seemed defeated, as if she had no more fight left in her.

"Mary Eve, you did everything humanly possible to save those children. You put your own life on the line to save them. You walked through enemy fire and offered yourself to the Viets so your charges could be free. The Vietnamese lied to you. It's not your fault."

She looked at him, tears flowing again. "If it isn't my fault, why do I feel like I want to die!"

"Your children did not die, why should you? Your children are back in their culture, they will adapt, they will grow and they will be a part of the new Cambodia. That might not be what their parents or you or your brother wanted, but war has a way of changing people's plans."

She watched him as they walked. She stumbled. He caught her. Mary Eve looked at him again.

"You think that I tried to save them? That I did all that anyone could have?"

"Absolutely. You did more than most of us would have guts enough to do. Never in a thousand years would I walk between two infantry units staging a pitched battle!"

A small smile broke through her anguish.

"I did that, didn't I?"

"You sure did. It was crazy, it was marvelous and it was damn heroic. You did what you thought would save your children. You should always remember that."

She shrugged, moved his hand away from her shoulder, and caught it in her hand.

"I guess you may be right." She wiped the tears from her cheeks and blew her nose. "But I still feel so sad that I can't get those children to freedom."

"They could have made it to Thailand and still starved there. There won't be enough food or clothes across the border for a half million refugees. It just might be better for the children to stay here."

"Oh, Lord, I hope so!" It was a prayer from Mary Eve.

They walked for a time without saying anything. Her hand held his in a tight grasp, as if it were her only anchor, her single contact with the outside, friendly world.

"Logically, we have about one chance in fifty of ever walking out of here, Stone. You know that, of course," she said finally.

"Maybe on in a hundred, but we have to try. I'm not about to give up and go back to a Viet P.O.W. camp."

"You've been there before?" she asked.

"Yes. I won't go back. Neither will the other military with us. Your life with the Viets would be even more unpleasant," he answered.

"At least, they didn't rape me. Vinh wanted to save me for himself. But first he had to have his bath and dinner. Then, you and Mr. Wiley came. I don't know how I can ever thank you, Mark. I owe you my life, twice! There is no greater debt."

"First, we get out of Cambodia."

She gave a heavy sigh. "Yes, Mark Stone, first we get out of Cambodia."

She let go of his hand and walked beside him. It was a first small sign that she was recovering from the shock of losing family, friends, and her six charges.

They walked for two more hours. Stone estimated that they were ten miles from the Viet base camp. Everyone was weary, so he called a halt. They found a small rise so they could see the river and the trail north. Stone stood the first watch. It was nearing midnight when they settled down. He would call Hog at three and get three hours of sleep before dawn.

Stone neither saw nor heard anything during his watch. He called Hog at three and the big man came awake at a touch. His hand lifted a long-barreled .357, centering it on Stone's chest.

"Yeah—hi, Sarge. My watch?"

The leader turned the sentry duty over to Hog Wiley who stretched, then floated to the edge of the small clearing, and checked out the silent water and the trail both ways. He was ready.

When Stone woke up the next time, it was to the prick of a knife at his throat. He came back to reality quickly but did not move. A Cambodian spoke rapidly and Stone opened his eyes. Three gaunt, dirty, Cambodian river rats stood over the group. Each man held an AK-47i and grinned at the sudden wealth of booty.

Stone looked for Hog Wiley, but the big man who had been on guard was not to be seen.

Mary Eve lay beside Stone. She sat up in the coolness of the dawn. "River bandits," she said softly. "They run the river, hide from the patrol boats, and prey on anyone they can find who has fewer guns than they do."

An angry Cambodian bent and slapped her, whispered something, and put one finger across his lips.

Loughlin and the two P.O.W.'s slept on. The two Cambodian guerrillas in Stone's' group were squatting with two of the bandits. They smoked a native tobacco and chewed betel nuts.

Stone thought how simple it was for these people to change sides, to shift loyalties! But then the threat of sudden death is always a powerful force.

The bandits tied Stone and Mary Eve with their hands behind their backs, then looted their packs. At last, they decided simply to take both the packs. They turned to work on the three men still sleeping. Each had used his pack as a pillow.

Stone tensed, trying to figure a way out of this mess. The Cambodians on his rescue team evidently were of no help. Stone had his hands tied behind his back and no weapon. Hog Wiley was missing, and the three other members of their party were about to be rudely awakened.

Suddenly, the jungle rang with a hellish, wild, screeching roar of anger. Hog Wiley stepped from behind a large teak tree and pounded three shots from his .357 pistol. Two of the rounds ripped into the bandits. The third river bandit dived sideways.

Quicker than Stone thought possible, the smallest of the Cambodian guerrillas surged six feet to the rolling bandit. He dived at the man, a knife flashing in one hand. The blade whipped down, and before the bandit could scream out his terror, the knife had sliced across his throat, cutting both carotid arteries and his windpipe. He died in a gurgling of blood and red froth that spewed on to the green jungle floor.

The second Cambodian guerrilla stood over the two bandits who had been shot. One was dead; the other lifted a hand for help. The guerrilla raised his boot and stomped twice on the struggling man's throat. The bandit tried to suck in a breath, and it was his last as the small fighter dropped on the bandit's chest, driving his knife six inches into the racing heart. The Cambodian anti-Communist guerrilla withdrew his knife and checked to be sure the other two bandits were dead.

Hog Wiley left the tree, walked toward them, stumbled the last few steps, and fell in front of Stone, unconscious. Only then did they see how Hog's right hand had been holding a ten-inch slash across his stomach. When his hand fell away, blood gushed out.

Chapter Fifteen

Mary Eve jumped to Hog's side before anyone else moved.

"Untie my hands! He needs help. Quick!"

Loughlin surged up and cut the ropes binding her hands. She looked at Hog's wound.

"Do we have a first aid kit? Bandages? T-shirts? We don't have much time!" She put her hands directly on the wound, pressing the bleeding flesh together, holding the sliced abdomen under her bare hands using them as bandages. Blood curled around her fingers and ran down her arm.

Loughlin pulled the first aid kit from Stone's pack, then dug two clean T-shirts from his own pack. They were white. She took them, folded one until she had several thicknesses, and then pressed the cloth directly against the wound. She held both hands on top of the cloth, pressing down and trying to stop the bleeding with pressure alone.

"Fold the other shirt the same way," she commanded Loughlin. "We need more of these, white ones if you have them. Come on! Come on! Don't just gawk—hurry!"

The Cambodians untied Stone who found another white shirt, then some two-inch bandages in his pack. He laid them out for Mary Eve.

She turned to Stone, one hand rubbing her cheek and leaving a smear of Hog's blood.

"Do we have any sutures, any surgical needles?"

Stone shook his head.

"Tape? I could use a roll of half-inch tape."

He found some in the first aid kit.

Slowly she got the bleeding to slow down, but not to stop. She took off the first folded shirt and told one of the Cambodians to run to the river and wash it. At the same time she looked at the wound.

"One intestine was grazed by the knife, but not too badly. No major arteries have been cut; that is a stroke of luck. We could use a ton of antibiotics." She put the white shirt compress on the ten-inch slash and blinked. Loughlin wiped the sweat from her eyes with a handkerchief.

"Thank you. Now, what medications do you have in that little first aid kit? Anything?"

Stone read off the labels. They were all long-lasting types. No penicillin, no antibiotics. There was sulfa. She asked for it. Stone tore open the aluminum foil packet and laid it on Hog's chest.

Loughlin had folded a third shirt and now she asked for it.

"I'll take this one off, sprinkle the sulfa in there, and then you put the other folded shirt compress on the wound just the way I have this one. Do you understand?"

"Yes, miss."

"Now, Mr. Loughlin!"

As he put the compress on the wound, she wiped her hands on her trousers and shirt and then picked up the tape.

"Knife!" she said sharply.

She peeled off six inches of tape and held it. Stone cut it with his knife. She placed the tape over the compress, fastening the ends securely to Hog's skin.

They had used the last of the tape by the time the compress was firmly in place.

The Cambodian came back with the first two shirts washed to a dull gray-brown. They were the color of the river. She took the knife, sliced the shirts, tore them into strips three inches wide, and then tied them together with square knots.

Loughlin pulled up Hog's shirt and held him off the ground as Mary Eve wound the strips of improvised bandages around his chest and back, further anchoring the big compress in place.

Stone had cut up the second shirt and tied the strips together by the time she needed them. She looked at Hog's head and sighed.

"He was also hit on the temple. Minor concussion, I'd guess." She stared at Hog and pursed her lips. "Nothing to do for that, I'm afraid. He should have rest. How soon do we have to move?" she asked, concern tinging her words with worry.

"You told us these men were river bandits," Stone said. "They must have a boat. If we could find it..."

Mary Eve closed her eyes, chastising herself. She spoke sharply to the two Cambodians. They ran quickly to the river.

"They will find it—no matter how well it's hidden. We should have our boat—and a motor. I'm not sure how soon Mr. Wiley will regain consciousness. Do we have any smelling salts?"

There was a small vial in the first aid kit. She looked at the label, broke it open, and uncapped it, before passing it back and forth under Hog's nose. He shook his his head, frowned; then his eyes came open.

"What the hell?"

The men cheered.

"You've been attacked, Mr. Wiley, and left for dead, but we fooled them, didn't we? You have a bang on the head and a serious slash on your abdomen. I don't think you should walk. We can carry you to the boat."

"Yeah, fine, Doc. Don't feel too damn wonderful." He started to drop into unconsciousness.

"No!" She used the smelling salts again and Hog growled. "You must stay awake until we get you in the boat. How does your head feel?"

"Like somebody used it for a bowling ball. It hurts like hell, but that's nothing compared to the guy carving up my guts."

"Good, lots of spunk. That will help."

A shout went up from the riverbank. A few moments later one of the Cambodians hurried back and talked to Mary Eve.

"Well, good news. They have found the boat. It's large enough for all of us and there is quite a stock of food that will be handy for the next day or two. We should be moving down there right away, Sergeant Stone."

He smiled and waved the men over to where he stood near Hog.

"He should be kept upright if possible," Mary Eve said. "Piggyback might be best. Can any of you carry him?"

Loughlin said he could. Patterson laughed and pushed him aside.

"You stand him up, guys. I'm the pack rat around here. You short guys wouldn't get him halfway to the water."

They hoisted Hog to his feet and draped him over Patterson, who took his arms over his shoulders. They told Hog to lift his feet and lock them around the tall man's legs.

When the full weight of Hog hit Patterson, he almost collapsed, but he staggered and then began to move to the river the way the Cambodians directed. Stone and Loughlin went along, each supporting one of Hog's big thighs, trying to lessen the load.

It took them ten minutes to get the fifty yards to the water. In a small creek that flowed into the Mekong, they found the boat. It was a Chinese junk, about thirty feet long. It rode low in the water and half of the deck was covered with a woven bamboo top. On the back was a twenty horse-power outboard motor. Two cans of gasoline sat nearby.

They struggled to get Hog over the rail and then laid him on one of the bunks under the forward roof. One side of the bandage pulled loose, and a flood of blood poured out, staining the blankets. Mary Eve stopped most of the bleeding, then sprinkled on more sulfa, and fixed the bandage in place.

The Cambodians were the sailors. They checked the boat, made sure everyone was on board, and then got the motor running. It started on the third pull. They untied the boat from a tree and angled the craft upstream.

Mary Eve told them to go as straight as possible across the river.

Stone braced himself as the outboard revved and slanted them almost due north in the sluggish water next to the shore. When they had gone a hundred yards, the Cambodian with the tiller angled them into the stronger current at forty-five degrees. Stone could see the waters snatch the small craft and slam it downstream.

The angle was not enough. They would be two or three miles downstream before they got across.

But they would make it to the other side; that was the first important step. He left the navigation to the Cambodians and then saw Loughlin with a CAR-15 across his lap as he sat on the bow. Transport, security all set. Time for sick bay.

Hog was still awake.

"Don't know where the hell them guys came from," Hog

said. "I never even saw them."

"Hey, don't worry about it," Stone countered. "We beat them. Hell, you beat them. We got their boat and we're going to be across this big puddle before you know it."

"You bring my 357?"

"Damn right, and your left leg, also your pack. You're covered; don't worry about it. Just ease back and relax. We'll think about the next step when we get to it. Right now just rest."

"Who the hell patched me up? That broad?"

"True, and neatly done. She's also a registered nurse. You could have bought the farm right there with almost no problem."

"Might still, man. I don't feel much like fighting with anybody."

"Sounds too good to be true," Stone joked. "You'll get over it. Now, have a nap."

He left and found Mary Eve facing into the wind, watching the mighty Mekong as they inched across it and were swept unavoidably downstream.

She turned and looked at him for a moment and then glanced back at the river. The distant shoreline was not yet in sight through the early morning fog over the water.

"You didn't tell me you were a medical missionary too."

"No one asked me."

"What about Hog?"

"He should not walk, not a step. There are some big muscles in his torso that need medical attention. Walking will tear them more. The severed ones will draw back so far they never will stretch out again. He should be flat on his back until he can be operated on."

"Could you do it?"

She shot him a look, then let it slide away. "I could repair some of the damage, if I had the right equipment, anesthesia, some good lights, instruments, needles, sutures, and help.

Which is to say no, we can't do it in Cambodia."

"So the answer to our transporting Hog once we reach shore is a litter or a cart."

"Yes, and either has added risks. We will be limited to the trails and roads."

"So could you ask the boatman to let us drift downstream when we get close to the far shore? We have to find a small village where they can go in and buy, beg, or steal a cart. It shouldn't be too hard along the river."

"Why not trade the boat and the food we can't carry for a cart?" she asked.

"Good idea. Did you get some of the fruit to eat? There's plenty for all of us."

"Yes, I ate what I wanted. There is probably other loot hidden on board that the pirates have been saving to sell at a village or town."

"The other Cambodian has been checking that out," Stone said. "I've been watching him. I'm sure he'll tell you what he has found."

"It's all stolen property," she said.

"Yes, and probably with blood on it, but it's ours now, and it's all we have."

Stone went to the man at the motor. They were edging out of the fast current, so they should be approaching the far shore. Mary Eve came and spoke quietly with the Cambodian. He nodded, smiled, and then spoke several sentences.

Stone looked at Mary Eve.

"He said he has been to this part of the Mekong many times before. There is a town of about two hundred people a little farther south. He says he can trade the boat for a good cart and water buffalo. This kind of big boat is worth three or four beasts and carts. Easy to do, but we may need to wait until the middle of the morning when the market is busy."

"Is the town big enough to have an army unit stationed there?" Stone asked.

After she translated, the Cambodian shook his head and spoke to her.

"He says they come through from time to time, but no permanent unit is there."

The morning mists lifted. It was just after oh-seven-hundred hours, Stone saw by his watch. He looked again for the far shore and could see it. They were moving quickly toward it now that the fast currents had passed.

The Cambodian chattered excitedly with his countryman and then pointed to shore. On a track of a dirt road, Stone saw a military Jeep racing to the north. He was glad it was heading that way so it could not bother them.

He wondered how far downstream the village would be. Hog's being so badly wounded put another serious crimp in his fighting forces. He relied heavily on the big Texan with the wild hair and beard. He ate two bananas and made sure the rest of the crew ate all they wanted from the store of fruit.

Mary Eve said the Cambodian had found a secret panel in the craft that contained a locked metal box. He brought it and Stone broke it open. Inside, they found packets of large denominations of dong, the Vietnamese currency. There were small sacks containing rings and brooches and some items of gold that would be valuable.

Stone tucked the packets of currency inside his shirt and then gave the jewelry to the woman.

"For your church collection," he said.

"Oh, no, I couldn't. That's stolen property. That is blood money; they killed for it!"

He took the small pouches back and gave half to the boat pilot and half to the other Cambodian.

"Tell them this is their half. We'll keep the currency. We may need it before we get the buffalo cart and head out toward the west."

She frowned but did as he said. The Cambodians cheered, and the one at the tiller, stared hard at shore, evidently determined to get the trade made as quickly as possible and check over the small fortune in his pocket!

Stone heard it before the rest. He looked across the waters and slightly downstream. The binoculars showed it to be exactly what he feared: a Vietnamese river patrol boat with a man already at the forward machine gun. As he watched, he could tell the boat was on the far side of the river more than a half mile away, but he was not certain if it had turned toward them or not. In another five minutes he would know.

Stone spoke sharply and all who understood crouched down in the boat or slid under the deck cover.

He watched a moment more. The river patrol boat turned and headed across the river toward them. The man on the machine gun sat tall and alert.

Chapter Sixteen

Stone edged his eyes over the top of the junk's low rail, watching the Vietnamese river patrol boat power toward them. It would have to fight across the swift downstream current if it tried to blast straight across to Stone's side. The thirty-foot boat slanted into the current for a dozen heartbeats, then the bow swung around, and the deadly craft turned back toward the far shore.

Stone wiped one sweaty palm across his face. He and his team would not have had a chance if they had had to go up against the machine guns. Only some lucky, long-range shots could have saved them. Now, the situation looked a little less bleak than it had a minute ago.

He watched the patrol boat move toward the far bank and probe as it worked upstream. Stone would watch the craft until it was out of sight. It could always slant across the current and come sweeping downstream in a rush if the captain decided to come check out the big junk.

The Cambodian piloting the junk grinned and pointed toward shore. A mile farther down, there were the thatched roofs of a small native village. This was where they would find their new transport.

Mary Eve talked to the pilot for a moment.

"He says he saw the river patrol boat. It would be good to go to the village and tie up now; then the patrol would think us a local merchant of some kind. He will get right to the market and look for a good buffalo and cart, one with a top on it to keep Mr. Wiley out of the sun."

"Sounds good. Tell him to go ahead. We better stay out of sight for as long as possible. Tell him when he makes the deal we will make the trade a mile south of the village. No sense showing two hundred people that we're hurt and running for the border."

She and the pilot talked for a few more minutes; then Mary Eve and Stone went farther under the junk's top.

The boat came to the village quickly, for a stronger current swept them toward the shore.

The Cambodians brought in the junk at the outer end of a lopsided pier that slanted downstream in the shallow water. One of the Cambodians jumped to the pier, tied up the boat, and continued into the village.

Stone watched through slots in the front of the cover and looked toward the far shore, alert for any sudden change of plans by the river patrol boat.

Mary Eve tended Hog. He had dropped into a rough sleep, shouting and rolling, and twice they had to hold him down so he would not drop off the bunk. Now he began to sweat, and she put her hand to his forehead.

"A fever has started," she told Stone. "It has come much quicker than I thought it would. He needs medications we don't have."

"Would there be any in the village?"

She shook her head. "They are lucky if they have aspirin these days. Antibiotics are unknown, so are doctors except for a scattered few and those in the army."

She sat on the second bunk beside Stone.

"He's going to get worse quickly. Within twenty-four hours Mr. Wiley will be in serious trouble."

Stone slammed his fist into the thin padding over the bunks. It hurt but the pain could not touch what was happening to Hog.

"I won't let him die!" Stone said. "I didn't bring him halfway around the world just to see him die of fever and infection!"

"We'll come up with something, Stone," Loughlin said.

"What? An air taxi? A helicopter to take him to a hospital? Maybe a state police escort down the freeway into Bangkok and a real hospital!"

"Easy, Mark, easy," Mary Eve said.

"Easy, hell! I've never lost a man out here. He's one of my best; he's my right arm. He can do things most men would cringe at even trying."

Loughlin passed around a basked of fruit. Stone took something that was red on the outside and firm inside. A cross between an apple and a plum maybe. He ate it, his mind charging around and around, trying to come up with some magic solution to his transport problem. There simply wasn't one.

Loughlin had been watching for the patrol boat. It hadn't showed. He called to Stone who came up from the bunk and looked out the side at the pier. He saw only one man running back along the rickety affair. He was their Cambodian. He crawled onboard grinning and waved at Mary Eve.

He gave her the story. She told Stone.

"He thinks he has been extremely fortunate. A man in the village is transporting his family downriver to the old Saigon. He can go ten times as fast by boat, especially one with a motor. He says he knows it is stolen, and he hopes it was taken from river bandits. He will want one AK-47 and fifty rounds of ammunition along with the boat. He says he must be able to defend himself against bandits. He will drive the cart along the riverbank so you can see it before you close the sale. The cart is covered and has a real American mattress! Plenty of room for two, plus many goods."

The Cambodian pointed to the roadway along the shore. Stone checked with the binoculars. The water buffalo was young and strong; the cart was the typical two-wheel affair with an eight-foot body covered by a tarp across a square frame. It looked weatherproof and better than Stone had expected.

"Tell him he's got a deal," Stone said. Mary Eve translated and the Cambodian left the ship and walked back down the pier to the cart. He vanished behind it for a moment, then the rig drove south, and the messenger came back to the ship.

"One mile down there is a small stream where we can tie up," the Cambodian said through Mary Eve. "He will meet us there."

On the short sail south, they stuffed into their packs everything from the ship they could use. Most of the fruit had been eaten. They had found a small axe and an entrenching tool. Both were taken.

They tied up in the small stream before the cart arrived, but remained inside and out of sight. There was little traffic on the trail here where it swept inland around a marsh the stream created.

When the cart arrived, Stone went for a closer inspection. He found it loaded with household items, but the mattress was there and would give Hog a softer, gentler ride across the ruts in the road.

An hour later the transfer of goods was completed. The Cambodian taught the merchant and his wife how to run the outboard motor and how to refuel it. Stone gave the man an AK-47 and two extra magazines. Stone showed him how to load a magazine, how to charge a round into the chamber, and where the safety was. Then, they pushed out from shore, let the Mekong catch them, and sailed away.

The pilot had inquired about the roads to the west and was assured that there was a main road less than two miles to the south. It would take them more than a hundred kilometers west into the heart of Cambodia.

The transfer of Hog had been the hardest part. Four of them carried him flat, and he survived. He lay on the mattress and smiled, then the continuing pain overwhelmed him, and he turned his head as tears came. They covered him with two blankets that they had brought from the boat, hung their packs on the inside of the cart, and moved down the road. Stone put Hillburton and Mary Eve in the cart. They had places they could sit. The rest walked behind or beside the buffalo, who took commands from the smaller Cambodian who had once been a farmer.

They found the road, turned west, and hoped that it was not heavily used by troops. After five miles Stone pulled them into a thicket and told everyone to relax.

"We need to do most of our traveling by night. We'll rest here until just before dusk, then move out again. Everyone get some sleep. I'll take the first watch."

After two hours, Loughlin came out to relieve him. Stone found a place away from the others, dropped down against a teak tree and realized the ground he sat on was nearly dry. The dry season had really come to Cambodia.

He slumped there, thinking about the whole damn mess, when Mary Eve came and settled beside him.

Her glance found his and tiny worry lines formed around her mouth.

"He's worse. I don't know why. It must be a fast-developing infection. Lord knows we weren't sterile when we bandaged him. The damn sulfa was probably outdated."

She took a deep breath that caught twice in her throat. "I'm sorry." Her voice broke and she leaned against him, shaking with sobs.

He put his arm around her and let her cry. His hand brought her head down on his shoulder and she continued to sob. In a moment he realized that he liked the smell of her hair. Then, she leaned back.

"I didn't mean to fall apart. I knew I couldn't up there where the others would see me. They expect me to save Mr. Wiley. He's going to die. It will take us ten days to get to the border in this stupid little cart. Where are the jet aircraft when we need them? This man can't live ten days without medication. It is simply impossible."

Tears filled her eyes again. "We're all going to die, aren't we, Mark? There is no way we can remain lucky and miss everyone of the patrols. All it takes is just one, and we go down from a dozen bullets, or we die from torture. I know I'm not being very brave. Mark, would you be offended if I asked you to kiss me? Not a lot of men have wanted to kiss me. I would appreciate it."

He brushed the tears from her eyes, then off her cheeks, and leaned down and kissed her soft lips. His arms were still around her. She sighed and returned his kiss. Then, to his surprise her mouth opened. But just as suddenly she broke away.

"Oh, my." She stared up at him. "Mark, I have never married. I've never even made love. Do you find that peculiar? We were always a very proper, religious family. Sex was for behind the closed bedroom door—but only after marriage. I wish now that I had let that nice young boy make love to me that night on the back porch when Papa was away. He might have married me then." She looked up at him. "Kiss me again."

He did, her mouth was open, and she sighed again. A look of wonder on her face.

"Did that . . . excite you, Mark?" She took his hand and placed it over her breast. She reached up and kissed him again, then lay back on the grass urging him on top of her. He eased up so he would not crush her.

"Mark, you'll have to help me a bit; but I understand there is nothing difficult about it. This is one small favor I would so appreciate." She unbuttoned the fasteners on her green shirt and moved his hand inside and over her full, warm, bare breasts.

"Please touch me."

Stone looked down at her and kissed her lips gently. "You're sure you want to do this?"

"I've never been more sure in my life. It's about time, it seems to me!"

"Mary Eve, one thing we're going to have to do for us to get very sexy is get you out of those pants." He smiled and kissed her.

Mary Eve Filmore giggled softly. She felt like a teenager again!

After her pants were off, she again put her arms around him, closed her eyes, and let one of her dreams come true. She had never known such stunning, marvelous, glorious surges of feelings! It was a whole new world to her. She reveled in each new sensation, wished it could last forever, then felt lifted to new and greater heights.

Later, they both pulled their clothes on and lay close together. Then, she sat up straight.

"I better check on Mr. Wiley." They went together, stepping over the Cambodians and the other sleeping men on their way to the cart. She had devised some straps to keep Hog from rolling off the mattress. He had thrashed against them, and the top of the bandage had stained dark red with blood where it had pulled away from the wound.

She loosened the bandage, stopped the new flow of blood, and looked at the raw wound. She frowned as she studied it in the failing light.

"Infection already, and his temperature is higher. See that bluish-purple spot. It could be gangrene starting. It can come on within hours in the tropics. I just hope that's not what it is!"

Stone left her to finish, went outside, and woke up the troops. They grumbled, then sat up, and were soon ready to move. Each carried a rifle with four magazines and was ready for combat at any time. Hillburton showed more signs of life. He questioned Stone's order that he ride, but shrugged and lifted himself on to the cart. That was some progress.

Stone watched each man. Loughlin was strong, sound, and alert, his eyes probing the semidarkness, ready for anything. The two Cambodians were still strong and eager. They had been excited by being near familiar territory. It had been like being home for them, Stone realized. They were hardy, ready for combat, and pleased with the bonus they had found in gems and gold. It well could be a fortune for the pair.

Patterson was starting to drag. After an hour or so of hiking, the ex-P.O.W. was going on the cart. The buffalo would not even notice the difference. He might let Hillburton walk for a while. It might help get his head straight.

Stone figure he was down to four ready combat troopers, including himself. It would have to do. Stone wished he could tell what was down the road. He had committed his final reserves now. They were tied to the road, which would make them much easier to find, and he had no scout out front. He called to one of the Cambodians and signaled for him to stay three hundred yards in front. He finally walked up to the point where he wanted the man, and the little Oriental understood. He grinned and waved.

"Any bang-bang, danger, come tell us," Stone said. He hoped the man understood. He had checked with Mary Eve when they went past the cart but she was sound asleep, propped up on the back of the mattress. She deserved some rest, he knew.

Stone walked back to meet his task force. He had two P.O.W.'s and he was going to bust his balls to be sure he got out of Cambodia with them. Even if it killed him.

For just a moment the dark thought blasted through his mind that this time there was an extremely good chance that this mission would kill him—and every person in his party.

Chapter Seventeen

They kept walking down the rough dirt road that was barely ten feet wide. It had no ditches, no hard surface. Many places were still soft where monsoon streams had sliced across. No work had been done to repair the roadway.

The small band kept walking.

The buffalo plodded along, head down, doing what it had been doing for years, no thought required, no decisions to make, only work to do and green grass to find at the end of the day.

For a moment Stone was jealous of the big, strong animal.

Hog Wiley cried out in his fevered sleep.

Stone heard Mary Eve talking quietly to him, probably bathing his face with a cold, wet cloth.

A chopper—he needed a damned chopper! That Jeep from the base would have helped, but two of the washouts they had already crossed could have stopped the Jeep. The roads and trails ahead would be worse.

Not even the large Vietnamese base back by the river

had a chopper. The Viets had few of them. They captured a lot of them from the U.S. at the end of the war, but that was eleven years ago.

He looked up as the sound of someone running came to him through the darkness. He held up his hand and the Cambodian stopped the lumbering buffalo.

The scout ran up to Stone and said something. He grabbed the scout and ran to the cart.

"Translate!" he said.

Mary Eve listened a moment.

"Troops coming down the road," Mary Eve said, "A lot of them! We must get off the road."

Already the cart was moving into the jungle, then into a small stream that was flat and open. The buffalo dragged the cart fifty feet off the road into the screen of brush, vines, and trees.

The men scattered behind the cart and crouched, waiting.

Rifle safeties were off.

Stone watched the road and heard them before he saw them. The men were talking, equipment jangling. It was not a combat patrol or a combat-ready outfit.

He saw a weary officer leading them. The man stumbled once, but he kept moving. He was probably thinking of the officers' mess at the camp up the way and on the other side of the river. No, he would be stationed on this side. He had a lot of troops going somewhere in a rush.

The Vietnamese regulars marched four wide and fifteen long. Sixty men.

Hog cried out in sudden pain and a moment later Mary Eve's hand muffled the sound. The lieutenant at the head of the column turned toward the cart, then shook his head in disgust, and hurried on. He must have thought now he was hearing voices in the jungle because he was so tired.

They waited for fifteen minutes after the troops had passed; then Stone ran down the roadway to be sure they had kept on going. They marched ahead, talking and laughing as troops do the world over.

Ten minutes later Stone's crew had the cart turned around and back on the road.

"It's not a matter of merely stepping into the bush now when the bad guys come marching past, is it?" Loughlin asked, looking at the buffalo and the cart.

"Does take more time with the cart. Just hope that we always have the extra time."

Stone had been over it a thousand times. Unless Sen grew wings and flew to Bangkok, there would be no help from her. At least, she would eventually give a report to An Khom. Her five-day trek would more likely come to eight or ten. Stone wasn't sure that she ever climbed out of the Mekong or on which side. She could still be trying to get across.

The unit that passed them could have been alerted by radio by the Viets. Surely, they had some sort of communications with all that was available on the market at reasonable prices. The western part of Cambodia could be watching them move west.

Stone put Patterson on the cart.

"Come on, Sarge, I'm doing as well as you are. I want to be out front in case we run into more of them little bastards. I still owe them."

"If we get hit, you damn right I want you on the ground with your AK-47 blasting. But right now you need a rest. I've got enough patients now. I don't want more. Get your ass in that wagon!"

Patterson shrugged.

"And Patterson, keep your hands off that woman. She's off limits!"

That brought a laugh. "Yeah, I could relax her a little; she looked tense."

They walked forward one step at a time. *How many steps*

in 220 miles, Stone wondered.

He walked up and talked with the point man. Everything was quiet. He went back and checked on Wiley.

The big man was awake and not complaining. Stone touched his forehead, which glistened with sweat. His temperature was higher.

"You got it made, buddy, a free ride," Stone said.

"Trade you," Hog shot back, but with less force than he usually showed in talk like this.

"Hang in there, pal, we're moving right down the road." Stone patted his shoulder and went back to the trail. Mary Eve walked beside him.

"His fever is at least 103. I don't have a way to bring it down except roll him in a cool stream somewhere. And we can't stop to do that. Mark, I'm getting worried!"

"Just before daylight we'll find a safe place off the road and then take a good look at him. Would it do any good to go into a village?"

"No. Any medical people were swept up years ago by one army or the other to treat the troops. There simply is no medical help in the villages."

Stone felt a deep, aching sadness. His long-time friend had little chance of survival. He remembered Lon, the Cambodian they left behind with the .45 automatic. Perhaps he had been the more realistic. He knew he had no chance; he took the quick way out.

If things got really bad for Hog, Stone was determined that he would offer him the same kind of option. It was the only fair and decent thing to do. He would never tell Mary Eve. She could not understand how a fighting man felt. He would not tell her until the last moment, and then he would have Loughlin take her away from the scene, carry her if he had to.

With that aching problem settled, Stone began to move back toward the point man. He had gone only a hundred yards when he saw the Cambodian sitting on the road. He was slumped strangely forward, and as Stone watched, he pitched on his face and did not move. Stone brought up his rifle and sprayed a dozen rounds into the jungle on the near side of the road; then he ran and dived for the greenery on the other side.

A stuttering of fire answered from the tangled jungle growth on both sides and just in front of where the Cambodian lay dead. It was an ambush!

He heard a yell from the cart. Stone pulled both grenades from his pack straps, jerked the pin out on one, and threw it hard so it bounced on the road and into the jungle. It went off with a snarling roar. He squirmed deeper into the thick growth and waited.

It was a damn ambush patrol! The squad was sent out or left behind to bracket the road and wait for anyone coming along to walk into the trap. It was the worst kind of situation for a moving detail.

From the jungle ahead, rifles kept snarling. Most of their shots went down the open roadway. Stone could only hope that the cart was pulled off the road as fast as possible.

He heard movement behind him.

"Terrance?"

Loughlin moved up closer to him and waved.

"One Cambode is down. They got him silently, probably with a knife. They left him as bait. We've got ourselves a small problem."

"You still have that scatter-gun?" Loughlin asked.

An AK-47 opened up across the road, slamming rounds into the enemy positions ahead of them.

"Patterson! About thirty yards up the road!"

The firing continued.

Stone pulled the SPAS-12 around from his back. He had carried it there for so long it seemed to be a part of him. He began working forward through the mire. Loughlin was beside him. The Brit threw a grenade and the explosion brought some screams of pain.

Another grenade blasted the far side of the roadway where the ambushers had been. No reason the Viets should move. It had been Patterson's throw that got some of them.

Stone wormed forward another ten feet. Loughlin had stayed on the edge of the road to give another fire base. He now chattered a dozen rounds into the enemy positions on Stone's side of the road.

When the noise of the firing faded, Stone could hear Oriental voices ahead of him. He raised up and blasted two rounds straight into the enemy positions ahead of them.

"Patterson! About thirty yards up the road!"

The firing continued.

Stone pulled the SPAS-12 around from his back. He had carried it there for so long it seemed to be a part of him. He began working forward through the mire. Loughlin was beside him. The Brit threw a grenade and the explosion brought some screams of pain.

Another grenade blasted the far side of the roadway where the ambushers had been. No reason the Viets should move. It had been Patterson's throw that got some of them.

Stone wormed forward another ten feet. Loughlin had stayed on the edge of the road to give another fire base. He now chattered a dozen rounds into the enemy positions on Stone's side of the road.

When the noise of the firing faded, Stone could hear Oriental voices ahead of him. He raised up and blasted two rounds straight into the jungle from where the talk sounded.

One voice raised high and keening, then faded, and ended in a scream of death.

As soon as he fired, Stone dropped down and rolled toward the road. Six rounds thundered from his side of the road into the spot where he had been. He had enough open roadway in front of him to blast three more of the 12-gauge, double-ought buck rounds into the spot where the firing continued.

The weapons went silent. Stone could hear movement. To his trained ear, it was a quick defensive response.

Patterson lay in the damp jungle floor and thought about the Asian Two-Step. No, they didn't like to come out at night. He worked his way forward another ten feet until he came to a big teak tree. He paused there, pulled the pin on his next to last grenade, and pitched it beyond where he could see the dead Cambodian.

The man had to be dead. Nobody lay in that position for this long unless he were dead or crazy.

A grenade blasted a hole in the blackness; then all was silent. Patterson had surged ahead just after the last shrapnel zinged past him, and now knew he was about twenty feet from where the Viets had been firing.

He breathed deeply and realized that he was out of shape. He was in no condition for a lot of this kind of combat work.

Now his ears became the most important part of his body. He strained to hear any movement. There was none. Slowly, he began to crawl forward. He eased through a murky pool of water six inches deep, then edged around a foot-high root, and snaked past a dozen two-inch thick, twenty-feet high bamboo.

His eyes were adapting. After the flash of light, they had dilated until he could make out forms and trees ten feet away.

He pushed his AK-47 forward and froze. Six feet in front of him a man sat on the ground, leaning against a tree. His shirt was spread open and his chest showed dark red stains. A groan seeped from clenched teeth.

Patterson sighted in on the man, and his finger began to squeeze the trigger when he eased off. More. There had to be more of the bitches! He scanned the bush. Left to right,

right to left, up and down.

He saw them. Two more Viets lay half-sunk into the jungle floor. Both were behind more of the ground roots from some lush growing tree. Two live, dangerous Viets with rifles. He searched again. For two more minutes he scanned the area. He could see the men plainly now. They whispered and looked down the road. From time to time they glanced at the man against the tree, but he did not seem to notice them.

Patterson saw the stripes on his sleeve. Their NCO was out of the fight and the troops didn't know what to do.

His AK-47 was on full automatic. He lifted it and aimed at the heads of the two Viets. One put up his weapon and shot four times down the road. There was answering fire; then all quieted.

Patterson made sure he had protection from any friendly fire, then squeezed the trigger, and held it back as the magazine ran down halfway. He swung the weapon to his right and sent three slugs into the wounded NCO. The wounded Viet was nailed to the tree by the rounds. He sighed and his right hand flopped down. Patterson saw what the man had been holding: a grenade with the pin pulled.

The smooth American-made grenade rolled out of his hand, and the deadly armed bomb lay ten feet from Patterson. He lunged behind a teak tree, mindless of the firing from up the road.

The grenade exploded and Patterson screamed from the concussion. He knew at once he was not hurt, but his head rang and his ears buzzed like a shattered nest of hornets. He had never been that close to an exploding grenade.

He held his hands over his ears for a moment, then stared at the battleground in front of him. The three Viets were wasted. He could find no more.

"Stone," Patterson shouted, "looks all clear on the right side of the road. I just nailed three of them."

Stone furrowed his brow, wondering what the hell Patterson was doing way up there.

"Hold your position and watch out for yourself!" Stone called. "We've got to clear this side."

He motioned Loughlin forward and they crawled, slid, and scrambled over the roots and past the trailing vines as they worked along the edge of the road.

Twenty yards ahead they found the remains of the Viet patrol. One grenade had cut down three of them. The shotgun slugs had wasted two more, and Loughlin's rifle fire had nailed the last one through the forehead.

"Looks like we finished them," Stone said, lifting his voice so Patterson could hear him.

"I got three over here down and out," Patterson said.

"Nine, that should do it. Let's go see the rest of the team down the road."

"Ammo?" Patterson called.

"Yeah, pick up any filled magazines. Looks like we're going to need all we can get."

Two minutes later they gathered at the cart. The Cambodian was told about his friend. He ran forward, picked up the body, and took it into the jungle. Five minutes later he came out alone.

"He had his own private burial service," Mary Eve explained. "Most Cambodians are Buddhists. They have a different outlook on death."

Loughlin looked at the buffalo as it pulled the cart back on the road.

"Our big buddy here caught a round in the shoulder, but it doesn't seem to hurt him any. Damn, but he's a big critter. Hate to have to buy feed for him."

"Anybody else get hurt back here?" Stone asked.

"Not many of us left," Hillburton said coming around the cart. He had an AK-47 and six magazines. "Sorry I was out of it for a while there. I'm ready now to do anything I can. I used to be pretty good with a rifle."

"Welcome back, Hillburton!" Patterson grinned. He grabbed the smaller man in a bear hug. That was when Stone saw that Patterson had three AK-47's over his shoulders.

"You looking to start a gun shop back home, Patterson?" Stone asked.

"Hell, no. First, I might need them case of a jam, right? Then I can always use a spare if one gets too hot. And I want a souvenir of this damn trek!"

"Let's get moving," Stone growled. "We don't have a lot of light left. And we're not sure what's up front."

Loughlin began to move out as point, but Stone called him back.

"Point is my job now. My fault, I lost the other point man, so I earned the spot. Loughlin, you're next in command. Get these people through to Thailand, or you damn well better die trying!"

Stone turned and walked forward into the blackness along the jungle road. He wanted to be three hundred yards ahead of them. It was the only insurance his small force had left.

Chapter Eighteen

Patterson was the one now trying to keep the buffalo moving. The big beast was not used to working in the dark and wanted to lay down for its sleep. Patterson had the knack to keep it moving and the caravan rolled along down the narrow trail through the jungle.

Mary Eve spent a half hour watching Wiley, folding new, wet cloths across his forehead, putting them back in place when he brushed them aside. He was still tied to the mattress and the floor.

He was unconscious, not just asleep. She wasn't sure why he had drifted off. It must mean he was sicker than she knew. A match flare had showed her that traces of gangrene had developed during the night. His fever was higher, at least 104. She wrinkled her brow in thought. She had no idea if there were any native medicines or herbs that might help with the fever.

She would ask the remaining Cambodian. He might know of something that would bring down the fever. As for the infection, that was a problem that was in God's hands. She had done what she could. Now she had to sit and wait, try to make him as comfortable as possible. Of course, the Viets might have some hand in that matter. Her lips tightened; her eyes showed her concern. But there was nothing more she could do.

She stepped off the cart and walked, thinking of holy things, humming a hymn, anything to take her mind off Hog's troubles.

Doug Hillburton marched beside Patterson.

"How long was I out of it?"

"Couple of days. You were sure no damn good to us in a firefight and we've had a few of them. Glad you came around now; we can use you."

"Hey, Patterson, we gonna make it?"

The tall man laughed. "You asked me the same thing just after we found out our plane was not going to fly back to base, then again just before we jumped. Hell, yes, we're gonna make it! I wouldn't have come if I thought I was gonna wind up in another damn P.O.W. camp."

"Yeah, I know. I won't go back. I borrowed the sick guy's .357. Know what I mean? If we get shot up, or if they overrun us and it's down to prison time, I'm for sure gonna blow my head off!"

"Been thinking about that myself, man. We're down some on fighting men. Hey, remember that little Cambodian woman! Was she a fighter! She was as good with an AK-47 as I ever damn seen."

"You say she tried to swim the Mekong? It's a damn mile wide." Hillburton frowned not believing.

"Yeah, she tried, and I'd bet a bundle she made it. Hey, you know you'll get back pay for thirteen years soon as we hit a U.S. installation! Stone says they usually promote the P.O.W.'s a couple of times. You could wind up with more than a hundred thousand dollars!"

"Hell, no way."

"Damn true. Say you make ten thousand a year. Thirteen years would be a hundred and thirty thousand greenbacks!"

Doug Hillburton started to laugh. He had enlisted out of the slums of Atlanta when he was fourteen. He used his brother's birth certificate. His old man never had more than twenty dollars to his name and he was a second generation, welfare trap victim. What would he say when little Doug came home with over a hundred thousand! Hillburton took a fresh grip on the rifle. There wasn't nobody, nowhere, who was gonna keep him from getting out of goddamn Cambodia and into Thailand where he was gonna ask for his money! Now, he had a real motive for getting his ass out of there!

The last Cambodian of the four they began with walked on the far side of the buffalo. He had his CAR-15 on his shoulder, but it would be ready in an instant. He was a seasoned fighter, had lived through dozens of campaigns and shoot-outs, and figured he would last for a few more. He listened to the jungle more than to the Americans talking. It was best not to talk in the jungle at night. But they were the P.O.W.'s. They were his responsibility; he had to protect them.

Loughlin walked a hundred yards ahead of the wagon, a kind of connecting file if they got into trouble. He could run either way to help. He had heard what Mary Eve said about Hog. He was not ready to write off the big man, but it looked damn bad. Right now the cart was holding them up, slowing them down and keeping them on the main roads where the Viets could find them more easily.

But there was no thought of abandoning Hog. It just made things a lot harder. If Hog didn't make it, then they would re-evaluate their position, their chances, and the tactics they would need to hike the rest of the way to Aranyaprathet, Thailand. But that was an if-and-when.

The damn bear of a man just had to make it! There was

no other option. Loughlin wasn't even going to think about any other solution.

A bird called into the darkness, and Loughlin looked in that direction with surprise. It was the first bird he had heard all evening. Was it really a bird?

Mark Stone heard the call as well. He had never noticed that type of sound in the jungle before. He paused; then a large bird beat the air as it rushed past him and flew across the road. Stone relaxed. It really had been a bird. He would know the screeching call next time.

An hour later the fringes of morning were touching the jungle. Light streaked in slowly, as if probing an enemy's position.

Stone looked for a stopping point. He found a small stream that crossed the road and vanished into a dark tunnel to the right. He explored it and found that the cart could be pulled up the stream far enough to hide it from the road. It was the best spot he had seen for a mile.

He waited there, stopped Loughlin and told him the plan, and the Brit seconded it. When the cart came, the buffalo stopped before he waded in the water again, but at last they persuaded it with a boot to the rear, and the cart was soon well hidden. Nearby, the ground lifted slightly out of the jungle rot and they found dry grass for a resting place.

They had been working through the broad plain, which was next to the Mekong and extended all the way to the mountains near the border. Here, there were a few low mounds and hills, created through centuries of erosion. They were resting on an area no more than fifty feet in diameter. It had some cover and a good field of fire.

Stone checked on Wiley. He was about the same. As the light came, they looked over his wound. Mary Eve lifted some of the tape and pulled back the compress. She gasped when she saw the inch-wide, blue-black edges of flesh all around the wound.

"Oh, good God, no!" she wailed. "It's spreading so fast! It will eat him alive!"

"How is his temperature?"

She put the back of her hand against his forehead. Quickly, she pulled it away.

"Far too high. I'm not sure—106 at least. He's burning up. That can kill him quicker than anything. The infection will take four more days to kill him. The gangrene another week, but that damn fever..."

"Isn't there something...?"

"No!" she shouted, cutting him off. "Absolutely nothing. I've been agonizing over this half the night! It's killing me, too. I'm supposed to save lives. Now, I have to sit here and watch Wiley dying." She put her arms out and he held her a moment. "It's so damn unfair! He was trying to help those guys get out, and now he's so close to death."

"I've been over every possibility," Stone said. "Steal a car, a truck, a jeep. Only I haven't seen one since we left the Viet base camp. Stealing a chopper would be ideal, but they aren't sitting around on every rice paddy." He gripped one hand into a fist and shook it in front of his chest. "Sorry, I didn't mean to dump my problems on you."

They went outside the cart and stood there in the soft morning light.

"Will he be conscious again?"

She shook her head. "Not for long. Just brief periods of time. The fever attacks the brain first, starts shorting out vital functions."

He patted her shoulder. "Right, now we have to think about the rest of us. You get some sleep. Pick out a nice tree and curl up beside it."

"I... I want to be somewhere... beside you. Is that all right?"

"As soon as I get things set up. You pick the spot; I'll find you." He kissed her lips softly and turned to where

Loughlin stood with the other three men.

The Cambodian said something swiftly, then frowned. "Watch" he said in English. He picked up his CAR-15, went to the highest point on the little hill, and stood by a tree, staring at the road that was hidden beyond the dense jungle growth.

"That's settled," Stone said. "The rest of you get some sleep; we're bound to need it. Looks like the jungle opens into a long delta of rice paddies. We've got to get through it, and we're going to be vulnerable as all hell. I'll take the second two-hour watch and then call Loughlin. Sack time. We sleep when and if we can. Do it now."

He turned back to where Mary Eve had been. She sat beside a tree ten yards behind the wagon.

"Wiley might call out," she said in explanation. He sat beside her. She leaned her head on his shoulder.

"Don't get me excited, Mark, or I'll never even have a nap. Just sit beside me and I'll be happy. You look like you could use some sleep yourself. You could use a good medical evaluation, soldier."

"I had just two hours sleep, just last . . . no, two nights ago. Sounds like enough."

He closed his eyes just for a moment. No, he couldn't go to sleep and miss his guard duty.

The stutter of a CAR-15 roused him, brought him up and running toward where his lookout had been. The Cambodian lay behind a tree. He pointed left and Stone saw three Viets running from tree to tree. The Cambodian turned and pointed out other places and shook his head. These were the only attackers whom he had been able to see.

Movement caught Stone's eye and to the left of the hill he saw Hillburton slipping from tree to tree toward the patrol. He had a rifle and two grenades. He stopped behind a tree and pulled the pin on a grenade. When one of the attackers ran into an open area and slid behind a log, Hillburton flipped the bomb twenty yards directly behind the fallen tree and blew the Viet into tiger meat.

The other two Viets turned toward Hillburton. Stone lay down and pounded off a dozen rounds at the two Viets, who quickly turned away from Hillburton and dived for better protection from the new threat.

The ex-P.O.W. waited and when the first Viet moved, Hillburton nailed him with a three-round burst. Loughlin had worked closer to the attackers and threw another grenade. It fell short but a Viet surged up to run. Hillburton drilled him with a single shot, slamming his head to the side and cartwheeling the corpse into the small stream where all of his troubles were over, all his problems solved.

For a moment the jungle was quiet. Then, the small Cambodian began talking so fast Stone could not catch a single word. They ran down the slight rise to where Mary Eve crouched behind the cart.

The missionary nurse listened for a moment.

"He says the three men below are only a patrol, scouts. There is a large force of perhaps two hundred men now leaving the rice paddy area a half mile away and coming this way fast in response to the contact the patrol has made. He didn't say how he knows there are that many men out there."

"Dandy. What in hell do we do now?"

"Maybe I should call down a miracle?"

"Part the red Viets, maybe, and let us walk through them on dry land," Stone said.

He whistled, pulling the men in the jungle back to him. He told them about the force coming. "We could dig in up here, but we don't have time. We could build some barricades, but they aren't going to last long against two hundred men. Any ideas from the troops?"

Hillburton spoke first. "What we should be doing is splitting up, every man going a different direction. No chance they could get all of us. But I know that we have a wounded man. And no way we're going to leave him." He spit on the ground. "Shit, no way was I going to be able to handle a hundred thousand dollars anyway. Where we forming up, around these trees?"

Loughlin began stacking full magazines next to the AK-47 he was using now. He had run out of ammunition for the CAR-15. The Viets would furnish the guns and ammo if the fight didn't last too long.

Mary Eve picked up a rifle, went to Stone, and touched his arm.

"You never did show me how to use one of these. I used to shoot a BB gun. Same idea?"

He said exactly the same. Then, he showed her how to take out a used magazine and to push in a new one. She did it once herself. The lady was a quick study.

"Remember to charge a new round in on the new magazine," he said. Then, he kissed her cheek. "You don't have to do this, you know that."

"Yes, I do. I'm just finding out about life. I'm willing to fight for it now. Where do you want me? Don't look so surprised; I have a new cause."

He put her behind the biggest tree.

Hillburton gave the .357 to Stone who looked at it with surprise.

"I figure Mr. Wiley might want this, you know, if we get overrun."

Loughlin placed the others, and Stone hurried inside the cart. Wiley leaned up on one elbow, pain etching his face and draining his strength.

"I hear a firefight? What the hell is going on out there?" He blinked, then dropped back on the mattress. He was still conscious and hurting. The look in his eye was strange, wild but still in control.

"We got big troubles. Two hundred Viets ready to nail

our tails to the wall. You want your sweetheart, here?" He held up the big pistol.

"Damn right! I ain't gonna be no damn P.O.W. Cock the damn thing for me will you, and be sure it's on a full chamber. Hate to have to pull that trigger twice."

"Figured." Stone saw lead in the right cylinder, then cocked the gun and gave it to Hog. "Take care, buddy. I got some things to do." Stone touched the big man, brushed some wild hair out of his eyes, and slid out of the cart. He rubbed at his eyes, which had teared, and looked over his troops. Six, including himself and an RN who had never fired a shot in anger. It wasn't much but it was all he was going to get. Time to get the party started.

Then, he went to the ground as a round slammed over his head. He ran, hunched over, to the small circle of friends and went down behind a tree. His small force was in position and waiting his command.

Out front he saw a squad of nine or ten advancing toward them. Another probe to find out how big a force was here. They must think it's Khmer Rouge; that was why they were taking it one step at a time, Stone decided. A three-man patrol made contact and was wiped out. If the nine man squad turned up dead, the Viets would move in cautiously with a company. It wasn't inspired tactics, but damn effective. Whatever worked was the best tactic in combat.

"Fire when ready," Stone said. Five rifles went off. He looked and saw the surprised expression on Mary Eve's face when the recoil hit her shoulder. She winced and looked for a target.

Then, Stone had his own rifle to use as he caught a straggler and blew a small hole through the Vietnamese's left eye.

Chapter Nineteen

Mary Eve sighted in through the CAR-15 rifle the way she used to with her brother's BB gun. The green-clad chest came in her sights and she squeezed the trigger. She jolted back with the recoil and stared below. The man she had fired at lay three feet away, his chest a torrent of blood.

She turned her head and sucked in a dozen deep breaths, then shuddered, and put her hand over her eyes. Her stomach rolled but she kept it all inside. She opened her eyes and looked back. She fired the rifle then, aiming at anything that moved and slamming out single shots in the area where the enemy troops lay.

Two grenades sailed down the small slope and a man rose to run before they exploded. He was dropped by bursts from the AK-47's the two ex-P.O.W.'s fired. The bombs went off and no more firing came from below. One man shifted, darted behind a tree, then worked his way through the storm of lead and past the trees as he penetrated deeply into the jungle until he was out of sight.

"So much for the squad," Stone said grimly. "The survivor gets back and now they send in at least a company with machine guns and some rocket-propelled grenades. If they have any sense, they will hit us from both sides."

"Let's relax," Loughlin said, "until they come back. Anyone get hit?"

Nobody responded.

Mary Eve sat up and Stone pointed. There was a tear in her green shirt and a splash of blood. She lifted it up and found a flesh wound near her left breast.

"Just a scratch," she said. "It won't matter all that much, will it? In an hour it won't matter at all."

Stone agreed. "Probably."

"I killed a man," she said softly. "I aimed at him and fired and he went down and never moved."

"Three of us could have had the same target," Stone growled.

"No, this one was mine, all mine. I almost threw up, and then I remembered Jennifer and my brother and Beverly . . . and I was glad I had killed him. Then, I kept shooting at them. I think I even hit some of the dead ones."

"Let's check on Wiley," Stone said.

They ran to the cart, which was on the opposite side of the hill from the attack.

Wiley had the muzzle of the gun pointed at the back of the cart as they came up.

"Don't shoot; it's Stone," he said quickly.

Wiley lowered the big gun.

"Three-man patrol, then a nine-man squad," Stone reported. "One got away. So we'll have more company soon. How you doing?"

"Been better. I can stay awake now. Doesn't hurt so damn much. But it's sure as hell hot in here already."

Mary Eve put her hand on his forehead. She wet a cloth and put it there and he looked at her.

"Thanks. You an angel or something?"

"Something," she said and kissed his whiskered cheek.

"Damn pretty angel," Hog said. Then he lay down again, the big gun heavy in his hand.

"We better get back on duty," Stone said. "Wait up for us; we'll come see you again."

They ran back to the hill. Loughlin said everything was quiet.

Stone and Mary Eve sat side by side behind a big betel palm. Her hand found his and held it.

"After this is all over, I want to . . . want to do it in bed with my shoes off." Her voice came as a husky whisper. He grinned and kissed her cheek.

"Deal," he said, then checked his magazine, took it out, and put in a fresh one. He did the same for her AK-47. "We might need these later on."

They waited.

The first probe came ten minutes later when a rifle squad ran into range and from good protection put the top of the rise under heavy fire. The friendlies there huddled behind cover and fired occasionally at the Viets.

Ten minutes later another ten-man squad began firing from the opposite side of the hill.

"Damn, Wiley is down there!" Stone grunted. He and two men squirmed to new positions and began picking off the second front. They had the job half done when Loughlin yelled from the first attack point.

"Sarge, we got a whole damn company moving in; they'll be ready to dance in five minutes."

"Save room on my dance card," Stone shouted back. He nailed two Viets with a burst of three rounds from the Beretta. They had tried to run forward. He threw his last grenade to knock down another Viet, and the two remaining men rushed back into the heavy growth.

"Here they come!" Loughlin announced.

Stone and his two men made it back to the perimeter to

face the larger force just as a rocket-propelled grenade exploded twenty yards short of the top of the hill.

"Stay down!" Stone shouted. He lifted up and emptied the Beretta at the advancing troops, then jammed a new magazine in his CAR-15. He saw it was his last magazine. He was almost out of ammo!

Through the firing he heard something different. Then, he tied it down: the *whup, whup, whup* of a chopper. It sounded like a Huey!

Four air-to-ground missiles slammed into the Vietnamese front below, mashing bodies, trees, and water-soaked logs into a new combination of mulch. The rockets brought screams of protest, and half the troops began to pull back.

The sound of M-60 machine guns rattled through the jungle as the chopper continued to circle overhead and pour fire into the infantry company. Another Viet squad picked up what was left of itself and rushed to the rear.

The chopper flew directly over Stone's position and he saw flashes of the camouflaged bird. A bull horn boomed into the noise-filled morning.

"Mr. Stone, are you there? This is a friend looking for a Mr. Stone with valuable cargo. If you are in the area, please get to the nearest LZ to your rear, away from the Viets firing at this hill, and we will meet you. If you have a flare, fire it now for confirmation."

Stone smiled. "Any of you cowboys got a flare?" Nobody did. "Loughlin, you and Patterson hightail it down the road and backtrack to that clearing we passed about a quarter of a mile down. Make a fire, make some smoke, attract that bird!"

"Right!" Loughlin shouted, and he and Patterson rushed away.

"Let's get the cart and move it!" Stone snarled. "We've got one damn slender chance of making contact before Charley gets curious and sends out a patrol with those grenades."

They ran down the slope, turned the cart around, and kicked the reluctant water buffalo into action.

But the beast had just one speed, slow and steady. The Cambodian led the buffalo, trying to encourage it to greater effort, but nothing worked.

Stone took Hillburton with him and formed a rear guard. They waited in the jungle for fifteen minutes, met with none of the Viets looking for them, and hurried down the road until they caught up with the cart.

"Less than a hundred yards to the clearing," Mary Eve called.

Stone ran ahead. He found Loughlin and Patterson gathering dry grass and heaping it on a fire. Stone lit the dry grass. It swept downwind sending up a black cloud of smoke.

Almost at once the beautiful shape of the Huey lifted over the trees and came closer.

"Mr. Stone, I presume," the voice said over the bull horn.

Stone waved his arms.

"Make way—coming in."

Stone waved the cart forward as well. The bird settled down almost on the fire. The rotor blew the flames in a dozen directions where they smoked into cinders. The doorway was partly filled with an M-60 machine gun. Stone ran to the side of the chopper, then back toward the cart.

"Everyone get on," he bellowed, still hardly believing the sudden reversal of their fortunes.

Loughlin stood beside the bird, his CAR-15 up and ready.

The cart came as the buffalo plodded forward. Stone sprang inside the cart and began moving Hog Wiley toward the rear. Patterson reached in to help. Then, Hillburton was there and the three carried Hog out of the cart and the six feet to the chopper's open door. Eager hands inside took the big man, worked him forward, and strapped him to a stretcher.

Loughlin's CAR spat out a half dozen rounds.

"We got company; move it!" he roared.

Stone pushed Mary Eve through the Huey's door and then rolled inside.

"Are we all here? Everyone in but Loughlin?" he heard affirmative shouts.

The M-60 angled out the other door began to chatter. Brass cascaded into the bird.

"Move it! Move it!" Loughlin roared. He drained one magazine, jammed another one in, and sprayed the jungle at the edge of the clearing. Everyone was in except him. He rushed for the door. The bird's engine revved and he dived for the opening on the side.

A series of holes appeared in the top of the chopper's fuselage where enemy fire sprayed it.

Stone grabbed Loughlin's shoulders and pulled him the rest of the way inside the chopper as it lifted up and away from the shooting. It swooped down to treetop level at once, moving away from the infantry.

Stone looked at his hand and found it sticky with warm blood.

"Loughlin's hit; where's that doctor?" Stone said.

Mary Eve pushed Stone out of the way in the crowded Huey, knelt beside Loughlin, and saw the pain etched on his face.

She saw his bloody right shoulder, borrowed his knife, and then slit the fabric.

"Lucky," she said, "it went straight through your upper arm. There's a first aid kit on the wall. Get me some compresses and some rollers and tape. Come on, you guys! You think Loughlin here has more than six pints of blood to donate to the floorboards!"

Somebody snickered. Stone chuckled; then the whole team was laughing at the reaction of their calm, collected missionary nurse.

She pasted the compresses on both sides of Loughlin's arm, pressing them in solidly to stop the bleeding. When it slackened, she wrapped his arm with enough bandage to keep the compresses firmly in place.

Loughlin looked at her.

"I say, are you quite finished with my arm?"

"No, I'm going to snuggle up with it. I don't want it to start bleeding."

Stone looked in the large first aid kit for anything that might help Wiley. He took out several small bottles of medicine and showed them to Mary Eve.

"Yes, yes, good thinking." She put down Loughlin's arm. "Sorry Mr. Loughlin, we'll play arm-to-arm later." She looked at the small bottles, selected one of Demerol, and looked at Hog. Then she pulled 150 milligrams of the fluid into a sterile needle and shot it into Hog's arm.

She looked at the other bottles, found some injectable penicillin called Amoxicillin. From this one she drew out a thousand milligrams and shot Hog in the other arm. The pulling and pushing and tugging to get him in the chopper had been too much of a shock, and he had passed out. The fever was still snarling along at full force. In an hour the medications should start bringing it down.

She sat beside him for a minute and saw that his breathing was a little slow but deep and regular. She went back to look at Loughlin.

"Think you'll make it, Mr. Englishman?"

"Now, I do. Where in hell did this chopper come from?"

Stone had the same question. He moved to the front of the machine and talked with the pilot. The man was from Brooklyn, a merc Stone had a nodding acquaintance with named Billy Brinkley.

"Explain it, Billy," Stone said.

Billy raced up a wide river about six feet above the water.

"The lower we keep, the fewer of the Viets know where

the hell we are. We've been leading them a merry chase for
a day and a half now looking for you blokes. A Cambode
woman, Sen, made contact. What kept you?"

"We forgot our invitations. We lost our radio when the
Viets shot up the other chopper just before we were to load.
All went up in one blast. How come An Khom knew we
were in trouble?"

"He told you, at least he said he tried to but you were
worried about something else and not listening. The words
are contingency and contact. You never noticed that An
Khom's birds keep a regular radio check with the home base
twice an hour. Just a fast check with a code name.

"Old Irish's code name failed to come through for two
checks, so An Khom put together this flight to come in and
find you. We located the other bird, and since then we've
been looking for you. I bet we've been in a dozen firefights
hoping you'd be on the ass end of one of them. Then, we
found the trail of the river bandit's boat and the buffalo cart,
and we knew you had a bad shot-up man. From there on
we stuck to the roads, and bingo. Second road firefight we
hit we find paydirt!"

"Yeah. You tell An Khom you have us?"

"Roger that. He sends his greetings. His bill will be a
bit bigger this time—to cover the other bird."

"True, true." Stone went back to his people and told
them how they got rescued. "Mary Eve, you sure this wasn't
one of your miracles?"

"My connections aren't that good anymore. But we keep
trying." She checked Hog. His fever seemed to have cooled
down. Another hour and she would know.

Patterson sat on the floor against the wall staring at his
hands. "Two hundred thousand dollars, and all mine! Wait
until I see that old man of mine! He said I'd never be worth
a dime unless I went into his business!"

Hillburton laughed. "Why the hell don't you go into one

of his businesses and bring me along at about fifty thousand a year?"

Patterson pursed his lips, thinking. "Hell, sounds easier than working. Just might do that. Let's keep in touch."

Stone sat down between the two former P.O.W.'s.

"You men are out; you're free as birds. I can't make you do anything you don't want to do, but I do have a couple of requests. One, this rescue mission never happened. If Uncle Sam knows about it, they throw me in a federal slammer for twenty years. They have prohibited me from leaving the U.S., taken away my passport, and especially refused to allow me to go into the far east. So you guys have never heard of me, okay?"

Patterson reached out and shook his hand.

"Damn right! We owe you a hell of a lot more than that."

Hillburton shook his hand. "Of course, I won't do anything to get you in trouble."

"Fine," Stone said. "The next one is a little tougher. When we get to Bangkok, we'll send you in a taxi straight to the United States Embassy. You should report in and tell them that you are U.S. servicemen who have escaped from a Vietnamese P.O.W. camp in Cambodia and that you want to go back to the U.S. and pick up your back military pay and the rest of your life."

"Some of the people you see there will be delighted and treat you royally, do anything they can for you. Some will be angry because they have been saying for years that there are no more P.O.W.'s in the three nations over here.

"Tell them you don't want any publicity. You just want to go home and start living normal lives again. That will cover you. They will want to keep your escape and your P.O.W. status as hushed up as possible."

"Hell, that's fine with me," Patterson said. "No sweat at all for me."

Hillburton nodded. "Same here, no problem."

"Thanks," Stone said. He leaned back against the side of the aircraft and relaxed. They had found two more. Hog was going to be on sick call for a while, but Mary Eve would watch him right into the best hospital in Bangkok.

Patterson cleared his throat. "This is costing somebody a hell of a lot. This chopper, the destroyed bird, the guns and the ammo, the guys you hired. Who pays for all of it?"

"We have some resources," Stone said.

"Hell, so do I. My old man will cough up megabucks just to see my face again. I'll need to know where to send the money."

Stone hesitated. "None of this would come from your back pay?"

"Hell, no! Dad will pay it. He'll never miss it."

"Your father really is loaded?"

"Damn right. At least he was. So now he must be double loaded."

"All right," Stone said, "I have a detective agency in California. I'll give you my address. I want you to memorize it. Nothing in writing. Then, if it works out, you can send something."

"Great. No sweat. I'll write you and ask for a bill! Christ, I can't believe it. I'm a free man—and a civilian if I want to be!"

Stone settled down again. Sleepy, damn tired. When did he sleep last? He couldn't remember. But they scored! Yeah. Good. They had brought out two more of the P.O.W.'s the government insisted did not exist. He had never felt more exhausted in his life.

Before he could think of another thing, he went to sleep.

Chapter Twenty

An Khom's rescue helicopter came across the border well south of Aranyaprathet, Thailand, circled, and came to Bangkok from the north. They landed at a private field that catered only to choppers and settled down near a hangar labeled BANGKOK AIR SERVICES.

An ambulance waited for them. The attendants did not even look at the other people. They checked Hog, said his temperature was down, put him on a gurney and into the ambulance. The sign on the side read BANGKOK GENERAL HOSPITAL. Hog was awake.

"Where the hell we going?" he asked the attendant.

"To get you well," the man said. Then the door closed.

Hog was in good hands and he must be feeling better if he could complain.

"His temperature dropped way down," Mary Eve said. "He's out of danger now."

Parked nearby was an old pickup that An Khom had loaned Stone to haul his goods.

They went into the hangar and quietly deposited all of

the weapons and ammunition they had in a pair of wooden boxes, which An Khom kept for Stone.

He retained only his Beretta 93-R and two magazines. Inside the big hangar building they found a modern office and men's and women's washrooms with showers. The two ex-P.O.W.'s stared at the showers for long moments after they stripped out of their clothes.

"Damn, I ain't seen a shower in thirteen years!" Patterson said. He grabbed a cake of soap and charged into the hot water.

Hillburton just grinned and began washing himself a dozen times.

Stone got on the phone, and before the men were out of the showers, he had clean sets of clothes for them and Mary Eve, suitcases, and copies of the latest English-language newspaper delivered to the hangar.

Stone showered quickly, went to a locker in the dressing room, and put on the same clothes he had worn out here three, or was it four, days ago. He had lost track.

Mary Eve waited for them in the small office. She wore soft gray pants and a matching blouse of pure silk, and she carried a fuzzy sweater she could throw over her shoulders. Her brown hair had been washed, dried, and combed. She looked delightful.

"I'm cleaner than I have been in months!" she said. "I had forgotten the luxury of a real shower with hot water! I didn't think I ever wanted to get out!"

"Is this the same girl I saw crawling through a swampy jungle?" Stone asked, teasing her. "You'll have a tub at the Bangkok Hilton."

"I don't stay at luxury hotels," she said. "They are a terrible waste of money."

"You do this time. There is a reservation for you there, all paid for, for as long as you want to stay. You'll want to call your home office to report in."

The Cambodian had already talked with Stone outside. Stone gave him one of the packets of Cambodian currency they had recovered from the pirates, and he hurried away to his home. He would go to Aranyaprathet the next day to wait and watch for Sen. He communicated to Stone that she would make it. It was her native country, and she had more spunk than any ten men he knew. He would share the jewelry and bonus money with her, the Cambodian told Stone with signs.

Stone glanced around. It was a much different crew from what had arrived an hour before.

"Well, if we're all here, let's go for a ride in style." Outside the door a stretch limo waited for them. The ex-P.O.W.'s marveled at it.

"Hey, I haven't ridden in a car for thirteen years!" Patterson said. He slid across the seat, turned on the TV, and pushed the button for the bar.

Stone put his hand on the man's shoulder. "Remember, you probably haven't had a sip of alcohol in thirteen years either. Stick to a few beers for a while, right?"

Patterson nodded and grabbed a can from the built-in refrigerator.

"Hey, they got Coke!" he said.

Mary Eve sat beside Stone and couldn't stop looking at him. They let Loughlin off at the inexpensive hotel he always stayed at. He said he'd have his favorite native doctor look at his arm, give him some pills, and do some stitching. He'd be resting a few days before he jumped a jet home.

Stone knew his home phone number.

They stopped the limo at the American Embassy. The ex-M.I.A.'s stepped out with their new suitcases. They both said they felt strange in the new slacks and sport shirts, and especially in the soft, new underwear.

They both shook Stone's hand. He asked Patterson what his address was, and the Air Force sergeant snapped back with Stone's Los Angeles street and number without any hesitation.

"If it works out," Stone told the smiling young man. "Now get the hell out of here and back on some U.S. soil!"

As the two men walked up to the entrance of the Embassy, one of the Marine guards came running toward the limousine. Stone stepped inside and they left quickly.

Mary Eve frowned. "What was that all about?"

Stone smiled. "When I bring back P.O.W.'s they always want to talk to me, but since I'm not here, I can't talk to them."

"That makes no sense at all, but I don't care. You're staying with me at the hotel tonight," Mary Eve said. It wasn't a question; it was a hope.

"If you'd like."

"You promised me a time with my shoes off and on a real bed." She blushed as she said it and he kissed her cheek.

"I'm never one to go back on a promise. But first we have to talk to An Khom and then go check on Mr. Wiley."

"Yes, yes, we should do that. I know he's going to be fine, but I want to see for sure."

They met An Khom at the pagoda. It was the same incense-filled, dark, and musty place of mystery as before. They stepped through the beaded curtain.

"Ah, the beautiful Miss Mary Eve Filmore," An Khom said, "I am honored that you have come to visit."

They went into his small office and he poured hot, green tea.

"I hear you were successful. That is good. The third man was deceased before you arrived. That is too bad. Just one day too late for him."

"Contingency. You told me about that?"

"Yes, but you did not listen well."

"The extra charges—how much?"

An Khom chuckled softly. "A man of action. Enjoy your

tea. Do you like green tea, Miss Filmore?"

"I have lived in Cambodia for ten years, Mr. Khom. If I did not enjoy green tea when I arrived, I would have died of dehydration."

An Khom laughed quietly, looking at her with new insight.

"That first chopper was valued at about thirty thousand?" Stone asked.

"It was old, not in good condition," the wily old Thai said.

"You're bargaining the rate down? I think we have a sponsor for this pair. Patterson's father is well off."

"But you do not know for sure. You have no agreement, no contract."

"No, but . . ."

"Then we play the game. Double or nothing . . . if you can collect."

"But the prisoners were there so we pay double. That was the bet. Just work out your costs, charges. I'll pay what I can before we leave in a few days."

"Credit is what makes business go, is it not so?" An Khom sipped his tea. He watched Mary Eve for a moment more. "Miss Filmore, you are a lovely woman. You remind me of my daughter An Ling."

They talked a few more minutes and then left by the front door of the pagoda.

The limosine was gone. The pickup truck sat in its place. An Khom knew when to economize.

"That was a business conference? Even for the Far East it was weird."

"We both work in fields where paper is not only a distraction but can get us in trouble. We deal in words, verbal agreements. It is enough."

The hospital was not the biggest in town, but it had a fine emergency room and well-trained doctors. Stone had used their services before. They found Hog on the fourth floor in a two-bed room with a small Japanese man who had fallen through a plate glass window.

Hog had just come from surgery and the nurse said they could stay only a few minutes. He was unconscious. Mary Eve asked the nurse several questions and told her she was an RN, and they talked a minute about the patient's condition.

Stone could see that the head abrasion had been treated with some salve and a dressing.

A large bandage covered most of his chest. Stone understood little of what the nurses said. They had to leave before Hog came out of the anesthesia. In the pickup Mary Eve told Stone what she discovered.

"The surgery took over two hours. There was considerable flesh to remove where the gangrene set in, and the muscles had to be pulled back and sewn together. He'll be flat on his back for a month, and then it will be another month before he can move around much. The wound went deeper than I had thought, but he should have no lasting problems."

"Best news I've had all day. He's on sick call for two months? Hog will go out of his mind."

"You better visit him every day; that will help."

"I will, or he'll break me in half when he gets well."

They drove on to the hotel and were shown into her room. It was beautiful, with a large bed and bath and flowers in a vase in the living room of the two-room suite. There was also a color TV set and a fine view from the window.

"It's marvelous! But it must be costing a fortune! I could feed fifty Cambodians for a month for what this costs for one night!"

He touched her shoulder and she came into his arms.

"Hey, you fed the Cambodes for ten years; now relax and enjoy a little luxury. Too soon we'll both be on a tourist-class flight back home. Let's make this a wonderful night to remember."

"First, I want to take my shoes off. How did you know my size? And these clothes. Who is paying for all of this?"

He quieted her by kissing her. Then things got more interesting . . .

In a few days he would be back home, watching and waiting until enough intel piled up proving the location of another P.O.W. Then, he would come back to Bangkok. Soon, he wanted it to be damn soon! Sometimes—when he thought too much about the Americans still in bamboo cages, still being beaten and worked like slaves and starved— he couldn't sleep.

He would never sleep well until every one of the M.I.A.'s was accounted for, and every one of the P.O.W.'s was freed and brought home. To realize that day, he would do all he could as the M.I.A. Hunter.